THE NEW FAUST
AT THE TRAGICOMIQUE

THE NEW FAUST
AT THE TRAGICOMIQUE

by
Brian Stableford

A Black Coat Press Book

Acknowledgements: .

Copyright © 2007 by Brian Stableford.
Cover illustration Copyright © 2007 by Michelle Bigot.

Visit our website at www.blackcoatpress.com

Dramatis Personae

Stéphane Moineaux, owner of the Théâtre Tragicomique, manager and leading actor of its company.

Marianne Jonquille, leading lady in the Tragicomique company.

Paul Damas, a young actor in the Tragicomique company.

Lillette Fevret, a young actress in the Tragicomique company.

Simon de Keramour, a pseudonymous playwright.

Comte Xavier de Farineux, a pretended connoisseur of the theater, Lillette's lover.

Doctor Emile Louvois, a positivist physician.

Madame de Vernier, the Comte de Farineux's sister.

Monsieur Léchelier, Madame Vernier's friend.

Monsieur Lavinière, the proprietor of an agency copying scripts for the use of actors.

Hubert Marin, a minor actor in the Tragicomique company.

Monsieur de Keramour's valet.

All the remaining players, including other actors in the Tragicomique company, Sisters of Mercy, a coachman, an amanuensis and numerous famous writers, have mute parts, although the actions of Alfred Jarry–a playwright and true connoisseur of the theater–speak louder than mere words.

1

The once-famous and highly experienced actor-manager
Stéphane Moineaux closed the cash-box containing the takings
from that night's performance of *Le Chevalier Malcontent* and
placed it in his office safe. He locked the safe carefully, and
suppressed a sigh.

He felt obliged to suppress the sigh because his leading
lady, Marianne Jonquille, was sitting on the other side of his
desk. She was probably too busy ranting to notice anything as
slight as a sigh of regret and incipient despair, but Moineaux
was a man who believed in keeping up appearances, even
when it was not strictly necessary.

"What, after all, did Monsieur Méténier do?" the tragedienne complained. "Was he the first director to have put on a
play about prostitutes? No–you and I had done at least half a
dozen in the previous ten years, and there must have been a
thousand produced since Murger first launched *La Bohème*.
Was he the first to feature a violent murder on stage? No–
every melodrama produced since *Le Tour de Nesle* features at
least one, and the greater number of them include two or three,
if not a dozen. All Monsieur Méténier did in *Fifi* was to
employ a cheap trick, securing a bladder full of stage-blood to
the victim's collar, so that when the throat was cut the illusion
was created that an artery is spurting lavishly. Anyone could
have done the same, had they not been concerned to maintain
a clean and tidy stage–and even though everyone does, now,
he still gets the credit for it! Has he moved on? No–he's just doing more and more of the same. If that's *avant-garde* melodrama, it's the only *avant-garde* in history that spends its en-

tire time in barracks, doing the same drill every day on the same parade-ground. It makes me sick. We, on the other hand, have put on a daring combination of the classical and the innovative in the last two years, and what do we get? People turn up their noses. To add insult to injury, we're forever discarding pieces of sticky red carpet and scrubbing gore-stained boards."

The Monsieur Méténier to whom Marianne referred was Moineaux's opposite number at the Grand Guignol, which had opened in the Impasse Chaptal, just around the corner from the Théâtre Tragicomique, in 1897. The Tragicomique had been in trouble before then, but the Grand Guignol's opening had certainly made a significant contribution to the speed of its decline.

Moineaux mustered the most reassuring smile he could contrive, and said: "We mustn't begrudge Monsieur Méténier his success, my dear. Everything that helps to maintain interest in the popular theater will be good for us all, in the long run." That was true enough–except, as Moineaux was only too painfully aware, that he and the Tragicomique were now extremely unlikely to be around long enough to reap any long-term benefits from the Grand Guignol's revitalization of public interest.

"What Méténier does is simply undignified," the actress went on, after taking another gulp of Moineaux's brandy. "There's no art in it at all. What will become of the true genius of our profession if all that audiences want to see is gouts of fake blood, vampire traps and all his other silly *special effects*?"

Marianne had begun to care a great deal about dignity now that she was of an age that made it extremely difficult to maintain a loyal circle of devoted and generous admirers. There was a time when she had only ever dropped into Moineaux's office after a performance to show off her latest cavalier, to demand that some upstart *ingénue* or clumsy scene-shifter be fired, or to proclaim her entitlement to an increase in salary. Nowadays, she only came because she knew that he kept a bottle of brandy in his desk. When the present

8

one ran out, alas–as it was likely to do within the next five minutes–it would not be replaced. That was how bad things were–although, as a good employer and devout gentleman of the theater, Moineaux would have died rather than admit it to anyone else. He would make up a good excuse when Marianne next went grubbing in his drawer for the bottle and failed to find it.

"We shall have to begin rehearsing a new play next week," the actor-manager told his leading lady. "*Le Chevalier Malcontent* hasn't lived up to my hopes."

"Nothing we've put on in the last five years has lived up to your hopes," Marianne observed, with hurtful accuracy. "What's the new one going to be. Not another foul-mouthed farce by that moron in bicycle-shorts, I hope?"

"Monsieur Jarry is an excellent playwright," Moineaux told her. "He is a little ahead of his time, perhaps, but I believe that he has a future. No, it won't be anything *avant-garde*. That's too risky. Nor anything classical; that's not risky enough. Something new, bold, exciting–but not too much of a gamble."

"You don't even *have* a new play, do you?" Marianne said, scathingly. "Time was when writers were clawing one another's eyes out to get to the head of the queue to show you their work. Now, they're all knocking on Méténier's door, despite the fact that the Guignol is the worst-designed theater in Paris and Méténier's as good an actor as you'd expect of a public executioner."

These comments were unjust, although it was true that Grand Guignol's premises had formerly been a painter's studio, and that its adaptation into a theater had been an awkward and rather unsatisfactory architectural adventure. It was also true that Monsieur Méténier's chief source of income before his theater's adaptation had been his service as an assistant to the public executioner rather than his parallel career as an actor. The Grand Guignol had, however, simply absorbed these colorful details into the proud record of its own notoriety.

The Tragicomique had had a long-standing reputation for melodrama before the Grand Guignol opened, but, once Méténier's reputation had taken off, the sort of plays with which the Tragicomique was associated in the public mind had been reclassified by the critics as "old-fashioned melodrama." Those that the Guignol put on, by contrast–which were as overloaded with grotesquerie and baroque comedy as they were with extravagant violence–had become "new melodrama" or "*avant-garde* melodrama."

Instead of the newer theater starting at a disadvantage, with a great deal of ground to make up on its august neighbor, Monsieur Méténier's establishment had somehow contrived to slip in front of the Tragicomique in the race for survival without ever having to overtake it. As soon as Méténier's production of Guy de Maupassant's *Mademoiselle Fifi* had scandalized its audience, the Grand Guignol had acquired the image of a sensational and up-to-the-minute venture, while the Tragicomique had been cast by contrasting implication as the coffin of the obsolete and outworn.

"It's no good blaming our plight on Méténier," Moineaux said. "Our fate is in our own hands, and it's up to us to get back on top. All we need is a single success. The Grand Guignol has been going for nearly two years now, and the newspapers are hungry for a new sensation. All we have to do is provide it. All we need is the right play."

"Which you don't appear to have," Marianne reminded him. She was forced to hold out her glass for a refill, because Moineaux had prudently taken possession of the almost-empty bottle. He hesitated for a moment, but could not bear to let her see that his desperation had reached the point at which he could no longer afford to provide his leading lady with a swig of brandy.

Moineaux knew by now that he had misjudged his response to the competition offered by the Grand Guignol as badly as he had misjudged the danger it posed. At first, he had attempted to rebrand what the critics dismissed as "old-fashioned melodrama" as "classic melodrama," reviving old favorites by Alexandre Dumas, Frédéric Soulié and Paul Féval. Then he had ventured into the reproduction of authentic theatrical classics, mingling them–cleverly, he had thought–with authentically *avant-gardist* works by the young Alfred Jarry and the even younger Guillaume Apollinaire. By the end of 1898, however, he had been deep trouble. He had told himself–and assured his employees–that things would undoubtedly pick up in the spring, but it was now May. He was on the verge of bankruptcy, teetering on the brink of an abyss from which no return would be possible.

He maintained his smile, however, as he looked at Marianne Jonquille across the desk, and hoped that his pretence of fondness was convincing, given the relative dimness of the muted gaslight and the quantity of brandy she had already consumed.

Twelve years had passed since Moineaux and Marianne had last shared a moment of passion, but the actor-manager continued to play the part of a devoted admirer. He maintained the habit of concealing cruel reviews from his fading star, although she had almost certainly read the one published in *La Presse* after the opening night of *Le Chevalier Malcontent*, which had asserted, with monumental unfairness, that Sarah Bernhardt's wooden leg had now acquired a greater skill for acting than La Jonquille had ever harbored in her heart, hands and brain combined. Marianne, for her part, did her level best to maintain the pretence, at least in the presence of the company, that hers was an unsullied reputation, and that the magnetism she had once exerted as a beautiful *ingénue* had ripened with time into true thespian artistry.

"I shall find us a play," Moineaux told her. "A good play... a great play... a *successful* play."

"How?" Marianne asked, bluntly. "I know you're in trouble, Stéphane, and so does everyone else. Even your oldest friends are giving preferential treatment to your rivals. No one sends promising young playwrights to you any more, until they've sent them to everyone else first–not even that scoundrel Lavinière."

Lavinière was the director of an agency whose typists produced multiple copies of scripts for the use of actors. He knew everyone, and heard all the gossip. He and Moineaux were old friends.

"I haven't seen him in a while, that's all," the actor-manager said, defensively. "If I drop in on him and butter him up a bit, he'll point me in the right direction. Not that I need to stoop to that, you understand. I've always had good contacts. I've always been able to pick something up when the need became urgent. People used to call it luck, but it's really a matter of knowing the business."

"Whatever it was," Marianne said, "you've run very short of it of late. If you're not careful, Méténier will be poaching your company as well as your audience."

"Have you heard something?" Moineaux asked, anxiously. "He hasn't been talking to Lillette, has he? Or Paul?" He guessed from the way that Marianne looked away, though, that she had merely been expressing the faint and probably futile hope that Monsieur Méténier might come knocking at *her* door.

"Nothing specific," the actress admitted. "Not that they'd be any great loss–*ingénues* and *jeune premiers* are five francs a dozen. You and I are the heart and soul of the company. All the rest are replaceable."

Moineaux made no comment on that, although the truth was that no one any longer came to the Tragicomique to see the once-great Stéphane Moineaux, let alone the ever-mediocre Marianne Jonquille. Young women did come to see the raven-haired Paul Damas, however, and men of all ages came to see the porcelain-complexioned Lillette Fevret. They were the most valuable assets the company had. If either or both of them were to depart, the Tragicomique's slide into ruin would surely become unstoppable.

Marianne's face had twisted into a scowl at the thought of Lillette. She still considered herself fully entitled to be queen of the green room, and was nakedly envious of the way that the gentlemen who gathered there before performances

12

flocked around the younger actress. The gentlemen competed for Lillette's smile more ardently than they had ever competed for Marianne's, and Lillette's current protector, the aging but highly-esteemed Comte de Farineux, gloried in his monopoly.

Moineaux had to admit, as he looked at the senior member of his aging company, that Marianne was more crone than queen nowadays. The only reason no one ever called her a witch was that she was as patently incapable of laying a curse as she was of casting any other kind of spell. Lillette, on the other hand, was a princess enjoying the heyday of her abundant charms. Although the days were supposedly long past when gentlemen fought duels over the favors of actresses, Moineaux thought that it was perhaps as well that Xavier de Farineux had enjoyed a fearsome reputation as a swordsman when he was in his military prime. Although he had put away his sword a full 20 years ago, no sane man would ever dare to contemplate calling him out.

While he formed that thought, the actor-manager's eye was inevitably drawn to the poster that had pride of place on his office wall. It showed him in the role of Lagardère in *Le Bossu*, in a production of 1876. He was not, of course, wearing the hunchback disguise that gave its title to the play, but standing up perfectly straight, brandishing his sword like a true *matamore*. He was wearing an expression of supreme pride and confidence that would have daunted the most dastardly villain ever devised by a steel-nibbed pen.

"It'll be a shame if you can't revive the Tragicomique, Stéphane," the actress said, draining her glass again. She placed the empty glass on the desk, obviously conscious of the fact that there was no longer any prospect of a further refill. "You'll go down with it, I suppose, I'm a free agent, though– and there are a hundred theaters in Paris." She was making an evident effort to sound confident, but she was not actress enough to convince herself that she really could find a position in another company.

There are a hundred ladies' licheries *too*, Moineaux thought, in an unlooked-for fit of sudden spite, *where raddled*

13

hagwives and disappointed amazons can weep for their lost opportunities and wasted youth. "Yes, my darling," he said aloud, forcing himself to be sincere in his mildness. "You could get work in any one of them, I know; it's only nostalgic sentiment that keeps you here. The Tragicomique isn't about to slide into the pit of oblivion, though. The mood of *fin-de-siècle* Paris is one of anticipated renewal, and I must take advantage of that. Everyone expects the old order to crumble away with the last 18 months of the old century, to be replaced by something more youthful, more zestful and more sensational. We must find a way to ride that wave of optimism. I must find us a play that strikes a perfect medium between the traditional and the surreal, the futuristic and the decadent, the classic and the innovative."

"That won't be easy," Marianne observed, unnecessarily.

"But it's not impossible." Moineaux declared, determined to prove that he, at least, was still actor enough to put on a good show of resolution. "There are dozens of up-and-coming writers enthusiastic to outdo Méténier's adapters. It's just a matter of finding one. There's still time to turn the corner, and to ensure that the Tragicomique will still be thriving when no one remembers the Grand Guignol as anything but a phantom folly briefly raised in the empty space where Rochegrosse used to commit his nightmares to canvas."

"I once posed for Rochegrosse, you know," Marianne said, reflectively. "He wanted to paint me as Sainte-Catherine. I told him that I saw myself more as Sainte-Thérèse, but he didn't understand, so Catherine it was."

Moineaux had seen the late Monsieur Rochegrosse's *Sainte-Catherine*, and thought it perfectly hideous, though by no means ineffective. Rochegrosse had been a follower of Gustave Moreau, specializing in mythological subjects of massacre and martyrdom. Given that Monsieur Méténier's own primary *métier* had been similarly drenched in blood, Moineaux thought, the Grand Guignol's theatrical productions could be seen as the mere maintenance of a tradition–an exotic continuity that the Tragicomique, which had always been a proper theater, run by a committed actor-manager, could not match.

"There must be would-be writers among Lillette's admirers," the committed actor-manager thought aloud. "They must all be avid to write a play for her, to demonstrate her power as an inspirational muse and their own devotion to her worship. But is there anyone *competent* among them? And if there were, how could I extend a tangible lure to them, while de Farineux keeps her on such a tight leash?"

"We're not lost yet, Stéphane," Marianne said, apparently feeling the need to leave on a supportive note as she went forth in search of further alcoholic reinforcement. "The censor will tire of being teased soon enough, and he'll take care of the Grand Guignol for us. The audiences will come back then—they always do."

This blatant falsehood gained nothing in the way of conviction from the dutifully theatrical manner in which the Tragicomique's leading lady closed the door behind her as she concluded her final sentence.

2

For a while, Moineaux reflected, once he was alone, it had indeed seemed that the censor's meddling interventions might come to his aid—but the Grand Guignol's several brushes with the law had only served to increase the urgency with which audiences rushed to queue for its new productions. The fact that people were never quite sure how long the Guignol's plays would last before being banned only added an extra spice to their appeal.

The brave face that Moineaux had put on for Marianne collapsed now that there was no audience to play to. He could actually feel his features sliding into glumness. His situation seemed hopeless–utterly hopeless, now that the brandy was gone, while he was still perfectly sober.

If I can't find a play in the next week or two, Moineaux thought, *I might as well jump off the Pont-Neuf and drown myself.*

After giving verbal form to that thought, though, Moineaux made a stern effort to pull himself together. He got up from his rickety armchair and struck a defiant pose. There was no reward in maudlin inactivity. If no budding melo-dramatist in Paris would willingly bring a new play to him in his present circumstances–not, at least, without first having shown it to Monsieur Méténier and being turned away–then he had to find another way of getting ahead of the game. He had to become a hunter, tracking down his prey by stealth and cunning.

But where should he begin his hunt?

Twenty years ago, he might have gone to take coffee at *Le Chat Noir* and eavesdrop on the arguments between the Zutistes and the Hydropathes. Ten years ago, he could have dropped in to one of Mery Laurent's *salons* to butter up Jean Lorrain or Rémy de Gourmont, either of whom would have had a swarm of young acolytes ready and eager to come up with whatever Moineaux needed, merely in response to their hero's nod. *Le Chat Noir* had gone the way of the old *Brasserie* some years before, though. Gourmont was a recluse who hid his lupus-ravaged face in the shadows when he received visitors, while Lorrain was in perpetual agony because the ether he had drunk as a stimulant had turned his intestines into a mass of ulcers.

The only standard recourse the actor-manager had left, it seemed, was to write to old friends in the provinces, begging to know whether there was some budding genius staging a new production in Dijon, Lille, Toulouse or Avignon–and they might not even reply at all, let alone by return of post.

By the time he took the door-handle in his hand, Moineaux's resolve had weakened and he was dispirited all over again.

Before he had a chance to turn the knob, there was a discreet knock on the other side of the panel. When he opened the door, he found himself confronted by his *jeune premier*, Paul Damas. His heart sank. Paul *never* came to see him in his office unless he had been instructed to come.

"Why, Paul," he said. "I thought you had gone home with the others. Don't you have some pretty *grisette* waiting for you in your lodgings? If you wanted to see me, you should have knocked before–I'm always at your disposal, as you know. A fine performance tonight, by the way. Had we gathered a more sensitive audience, you'd have received the applause that is your manifest due, but they were a dull lot, incapable of appreciating your artistry. Tomorrow night's crowd will be better, I'm sure."

"I thought it best to wait until Marianne had gone," Paul said, as Moineaux invited him to sit down before resuming his own seat behind his desk. "It's a slightly delicate matter."

Moineaux had reconstructed his brave face, but had not contrived to resurrect his smile. The young actor's serious tone relieved him of that responsibility, but amplified his hidden anxiety. There was, he supposed, a faint hope that the young man had merely got the wrong girl pregnant, but instinct told him that it was infinitely more likely to be a matter of money. He summoned up the attitude of pseudoparental gravitas that had done sterling service in 50 domestic dramas in order to say: "What is it, my boy? You can rely absolutely on my discretion and support."

"I've had an offer of a part at the Ambigu-Comique," Paul confessed. "I didn't audition for it–the manager there heard a good report of my performance here... not in our present production, but last month's adaptation of *Capitaine Tempête*. He intends to put on a version of Monsieur Robert's *Le Bouquet de Satan*, and felt that I... well, in sum, he's offered me 30 francs a month more than my present wages. I've been happy here, of course, working with you... but as you said yourself, the audiences have been a little dull of late, and the Ambigu always attracts a good crowd. I'm assured that the opportunity would eventually arise to work with Sarah Bernhardt..."

"You mustn't take assurances like that too seriously, Paul," Moineaux told him, speaking softly but severely. "Tempting promises are a tantalizing currency, but they often evaporate like mirages. Thirty francs a month in hard cash would certainly be worth taking seriously, of course, if you could guarantee that you'd receive it every month–but the Ambigu's company is much bigger than mine. The directors have half a dozen *jeune premiers* to draw upon, and there's no guarantee that you'd be working all the year round, and certainly not in prominent roles. It's a fine stage, to be sure, but it's not what it was in Daguerre's day–and with all due respect, La Bernhardt isn't getting any younger. Did you know that she's a year older than Marianne?"

"No, I didn't," Paul admitted. "And what you say about the size of the Ambigu's company is doubtless true, but..."

"You mustn't underestimate the value of playing opposite Lillette," Moineaux said, hastening to heap up a few more disincentives. "She has a great future ahead of her, and I'm planning to increase the prominence of her roles considerably. Naturally, that will require a similar increase in the prominence of yours. I'm growing old myself, as you're obviously well aware, and I'll soon be looking around for an heir to take over the company, and perhaps the theater itself. Hubert Marin's the senior man in the company, of course, but he's not up to the job; nor is Marianne, although I suppose I ought not to discount her on the basis of her sex in this day and age. No, the job needs a young man, with talent, dynamism and ambition. But it needs a man who's prepared to serve his apprenticeship in full, and to master every aspect of his craft. I've seen a great many promising actors ruined by their inability to settle, their insistence on flitting here and there in search of the best-paying job of the moment rather than buckling down and building a career. You could be a great actor, Paul, with expert tutelage and the right guidance."

"Thank you for saying so," the embarrassed *jeune premier* stammered. "I'm grateful for your confidence, and your advice. The opportunity to continue to play opposite Lillette would certainly be a golden one, if..."

"If?" echoed Moineaux, hastening to interrupt again. "Is there an *if* about it? Do you think that Lillette might be wooed away by the promise of another 30 francs a month? That's nothing to her while she has the Comte's money at her disposal. He dotes on her, you know, and she's loyal to me–fervently loyal."

"As she should be," Paul conceded. "But it's the Comte, you see, who's looking for a better position for her. She's happy where she is, as you know, but if he's not happy... in a conflict of loyalties, you see, she's be bound to favor the man who maintains her in the manner to which she's accustomed. She couldn't do that on the wages you pay her, even if it were increased by 100 francs a month. There's nothing for her just now at the Ambigu or the Gymnase, I understand, let alone the Opéra-Comique, but there's been gossip in the green room, put about by the Comte, that interest in her has been expressed at the Gambardi and the Bouffée."

Damn you, Marianne! Moineaux thought. *You sit there sipping my brandy, and don't say a word. Or are you too drunk even before performances nowadays to take notice of what's going on around you?* As the company's director, he was always too busy to partake of the social chitchat that preceded performances, and had to rely on others to collect salient gossip on his behalf.

Moineaux knew that he ought to feign indignation, and dismiss the pretensions of the Gambardi and the Bouffée as hollow shams beneath contempt, but he could not quite muster sufficient hypocrisy. He knew full well that if the Comte de Farineux could engineer an opening for Lillette Fevret at either rival venue, it would very probably work to her advantage, given the difficulties the Tragicomique was presently experiencing. He knew, too, that Lillette had the potential to be a far better actress than the sluts currently serving as tempt-resses-in-chief at either of the named theaters.

The temptresses in question would have their own pro-tectors, of course, who might well be bankers or businessmen, as rich or richer than the Comte–but they could not possibly match him for social prestige. Xavier de Farineux had been a hero in his day, and the awful fiasco of the battle of Sedan had not eclipsed the memory of his previous exploits. He had in-fluence beyond the scope of his pockets, rare though that quality was in Paris nowadays. If the Comte were determined to lever his own *protégée* into a company ahead of the resident *ingénue*, he might well be able to do it.

"What I have said to you," Moineaux told his protégé, suavely, "I shall also say to Lillette, should the need arise. She will be a great actress one day, with expert tutelage and the right guidance–provided that she devotes herself to work and her art rather than following the whims of fashion. Here, you have her talent to draw upon and she has yours, and you both have mine. It is a formidable combination, Paul–more formi-dable than you are yet able to judge. Broken, its parts might fade away into oblivion, but united, it might yet accomplish great things. Don't go to the Ambigu, Paul. I'm not saying that for my benefit–although it will certainly benefit me if you stay–but for yours. You're like a son to me, and I care pro-foundly about our future. When the moment comes for you to fly the nest, I'll be the first to bid you a generous farewell, but the moment has not yet come. Trust my judgement on that."

Paul's face was a study in confusion. His mental agony would have been appreciable in the fifth row of the circle, let alone the stalls. "I do trust you, *Maître*," he said. "I owe you everything, and I'm very grateful... but if you could only see your way to paying me a little more. Thirty francs..."

"Would feel like 30 pieces of silver if I were to offer them," Moineaux told him, "for I'd be betraying your future. One day, you'll deserve more–far more–than I can pay you, now or in the future, but if you run off chasing fool's gold now, before you've learned your craft well enough to be truly worthy of that kind of hire, your career will go off the rails in no time, I can't let you do it, Paul; I'd be failing in my duty as a father if I did. I insist that you stay–but I'll tell you what I will do. I'll find you a role, Paul: a role that will stretch you to the limit; a role that will bring out everything that's latent in you, and give you the chance to be the actor you long to be.

"Give me a month, Paul–no, three weeks. Give me three weeks, and if I haven't found you a role that you'd kill to win and make your own, I'll agree to step back into the wings and leave you to make your own decision as to whether to go off chasing silvery moonbeams. You can't deny me three weeks, Paul, can you? I'm offering you a real chance, worth far more in the long run than a mere 30 francs in the palm of your hand."

"Well..." the *jeune premier* began.

Moineaux cut him off, standing up abruptly and thrusting out his hand. "That's settled, then," he declared. "We've shaken hands on it, like true gentlemen of the theater." He seized the hand that Paul had half-extended without really meaning to, and shook it violently. Hardly pausing to draw breath, he went on: "Now, young fellow, you must go home. Get some sleep. We have another performance tomorrow, and you must be brilliant. If the audience is dull, you must do your utmost to brighten their lives. Don't thank me; just go." There was a hint of a tear in his eye as he bid the *jeune premier* farewell–a hint whose delicacy he had worked on for years. Before the younger actor had caught up with the flow of events, they were both in the corridor, hastening toward the stage door.

Moineaux had to pause to give a few final instructions to the caretaker, and was glad to see when he looked around again that Paul had carried on and disappeared.

"If only he *were* as easily replaceable as Marianne imagines," the actor-manager murmured. "Now, it seems, I must make haste to deal with the impatient Comte."

"What's that, Monsieur Moineaux," the caretaker said, although he had worked at he theater long enough to be thoroughly familiar with his employer's habit of talking to himself.

"Nothing, Jacques," Moineaux assured his employee. "I was just giving myself my own final instructions. Goodnight."

"Goodnight, Monsieur Moineaux," the caretaker replied, politely, as he moved off. Moineaux heard the old man muttering something about a bloodstained stage and the woeful inadequacy of his mop, but he knew that the words weren't really intended to reach his ears.

3

Had it been socially permissible, Moineaux would have called upon the Comte de Farineux that same evening, but convention ruled it impossible. Although Xavier de Farineux had been an individualist in the days when he was a military hero, he was nowadays almost as devoted to the rules of etiquette as he was to the appreciation of the theater. The next morning, however, at eleven o'clock on the dot, the actor-manager presented his card at the main door of the Comte's town house in the Rue Vaugirard, the Hôtel de Farineux, and asked for an interview. He was shown into a reception room and asked to wait.

Moineaux had already dashed off and dispatched a series of letters to acquaintances in Dijon, Lyon, Toulouse, Lille and Brussels, informing them that he had been moved by innate generosity of spirit and an increasing consciousness of the passing of the years to explore the possibility of extending his invaluable patronage to a deserving provincial playwright. He had requested each of them to send him an exemplary manuscript with all possible haste. He was now impatient to explore other avenues of discovery, but dared not do so while the foundations of his enterprise might be crumbling beneath his feet. He had to make sure that his company retained such force of attraction as it had, and the greater part of its charm, at present, was contained in the person of Lillette Fevret.

While he waited, Moineaux was able to study the portraits of Xavier de Farineux and his immediate ancestors that were hung on the walls of the reception-room. His father, grandfather and great-grandfather had also been military men, but the vicissitudes of history had ensured that they wore different uniforms. Edouard-Christophe de Farineux had been a colonel in Louis-Philippe's army in the years after the July Revolution of 1830, while Hugues-Gustave de Farineux had reached the same rank fighting for the first Napoleon in Spain and Egypt and Charles-Honoré de Farineux had done likewise in the army of Louis XVI.

The ensemble of portraits might have given the impression to an unsympathetic observer that the first allegiance of the de Farineux family had always been to the sword and the business of murder, and that they did not care overmuch who might commission them to do it. Moineaux chose to take the more generous view, however, that they were patriotic men of France, ever-ready bravely to defend their countrymen against all manner of foreign threats. They would probably have taken arms against the Devil himself–unless, of course, the Devil had somehow established himself as the French Head of State.

When the Comte de Farineux finally came into the room to greet his visitor, obviously having taken a very late breakfast, Moineaux bowed ostentatiously and said: "I have good news, Monsieur le Comte, which I could not keep to myself. It concerns our young *protégée*, the divine Lillette. I have found the perfect role for her, after months of assiduous searching. It is time for her to emerge from the shadow of Marianne Jonquille–who, as you must have observed during your recent attendance at my humble establishment, is nowadays more suited to maternal roles than leading parts. It is time for our nursling to take wing, and become the shining star that she was always destined to be."

"That is very good news, Monsieur Moineaux," the Comte said, agreeably but with a hint of acidity, "but I am not sure why you have brought it to me. You're not looking for financial assistance for the costs of your next production, I hope? May I remind you that you promised me when I backed *Capitaine Tempête* that you would not call upon me again if the play was unsuccessful. It was not successful, Monsieur Moineaux."

"You're absolutely right, sire," Moineaux told him. "The Tragicomique company has been very fortunate to receive your occasional patronage in the past, and I have been very grateful for your generosity. I make it a point of principle always to honor my promises, though, and I would not dream of asking you for further financial support. We gentlemen of the theater are not beggars to hold out our bowls, or priests to send round our collection-plates. No, I came to beg you for an altogether different kind of assistance. Lillette is a fragile flower, you see; she lacks self-confidence. I know that she is ready to take on the kind of role I have prepared for her, and I know that you are as certain as I am, for I've seen how closely you study her from your box. Alas, *she* does not know that she is ready. She will need your help, Comte, as much as she will need mine, if she is to take full advantage of this glorious opportunity.

"You are a connoisseur of the theater, I know, who has seen a great many young actresses, and have offered moral and material support to more than a few. I know what your talents are in the matter of encouraging young girls to blossom into mature women and mature artists. I came to you before I even dared mention the possibility of a promotion to a leading role to her, because I know that she will need your reassurance, your faith, and your tender affection, if she is to believe herself capable of seizing the chance and making the most of it. Indeed, it would be greatly to her benefit if you were to give her the news yourself. You might, for instance, say to her: 'I have seen Monsieur Moineaux, my darling, and he has asked me to talk to you, as your firmest friend and greatest admirer, and to tell you that you are ready to accept the greatest chal-

24

lenge of you career: to play a role as great as any that has been written for a leading actress in the 19th century.'

"She will very likely protest, and say that she is not yet ready to play any roles but *ingénues*. She might even say that she would rather take a slower and more painstaking road to fame, perhaps by broadening her experience in other companies than the Tragicomique's. If so, you might say: 'Yes, my darling, that would doubtless be the safer course—but those who calculate to remain in relative obscurity sometimes find themselves becalmed or bogged down despite their ability, while those who flit from theater to theater sometimes find themselves branded butterflies wanting in loyalty. Those brave souls, on the other hand, who are able to grasp the nettle boldly may find their latent talents blossoming in glorious profusion.' I think, Comte, that we can both agree that Lillette has a very considerable talent, and that it would be a wonderful thing to be instrumental in such a fabulous unfolding. She would, I think, be very glad to receive this news from you. She could not love you any more than she already does, but there may yet be scope for the quality of her passion to become even finer."

"You're very eloquent, Monsieur Moineaux," the Comte said, not bothering to conceal the sarcasm lurking behind his over-scrupulous politeness. "I'm not sure that I could match your skill with words—especially your propensity to speak in such long sentences—in addressing someone whose beauty and charm, I must confess, sometimes leave me a little tongue-tied."

"You need have no worries on that score, sire," Moineaux assured him, keeping his own sarcasm extremely well hidden. "Why, you'd have made a very fine actor yourself had your military vocation not destined you for far greater things. I've played many a hero on stage, but I've never been one, and I know that you could have stepped into my shoes in many a production and put my performance to shame with the sheer vigor and honesty of your representation.

"When I called you a connoisseur of the theater, sire, I did not mean to liken you to those gentlemen whose vast experience of boxes and stalls is unmatched by the slightest experience in life; you are a *true* connoisseur, who can judge a performance from every angle. Our darling Lillette adores you for other reasons, but she has intelligence enough to know that yours is an opinion to be respected above all others, a judgement to be trusted implicitly. If you tell her that she has your full confidence, as well as your affection, she will listen and she will respond.

"You and I can be the making of her, Comte, if we only pull together. I am happy to say that I can now provide the ideal play, as well as the right supporting cast and expert direction, but all that is not enough to bring a tender bud like Lillette into full flower. She also needs your unbreakable faith, your unlimited encouragement and your unqualified admiration. Together, we might work a miracle with that *fillette* that no other combination could contrive."

In fact, Moineaux thought, as he brought this florid speech to a conclusion, there was a certain amount of truth in what he said. Lillette did need coaxing, and her need went beyond the kinds of reassurance that a director could provide. A director had to be stern, to correct mistakes, to apply the whip as well as the carrot. Lillette was the kind of actress who needed a counterweight to balance that judicious criticism. She needed someone whose belief in her ability was absolute and unwavering, or someone who could pretend. She was very young, as yet–hardly 20–and would doubtless grow in confidence once she began to play leading roles as a matter of routine, but she would need her worshippers even then.

"You flatter me, Monsieur Moineaux," the Comte de Farineux murmured. There was an exaggerated silkiness in his tone, redolent with irony. He was a man who liked to be flattered, as Moineaux knew very well, but Moineaux also knew that he did not like that tendency to be understood and exploited by others.

"Not at all, sire," the actor-manager said. "I know that you can help me in this, and I wish you would, for Lillette's sake as well as mine. Will you do it?"

"What, exactly, is this wonderful role that you have found for my little dove? I should dearly like to read the play in question."

"Indeed you must," Moineaux declared, "at the earliest possible opportunity. That will be as soon as the actors' scripts have come back from the copyists, perhaps in three days' time. But we must begin *our* preparations in advance of that, Monsieur le Comte. We must lay the groundwork, dress the stage, and build *morale*. I cannot lie to you, since your expert eye has been scanning the stage from your box: our current production is not a success. I blame myself, entirely–well, not entirely, since I was persuaded, much against my judgement, to put on the play by eager backers that I hesitated to offend, and a playwright who undoubtedly has promise, if he would only consent to take wise advice–but the final responsibility is mine, always mine. At any rate, the play has not gone well, despite the best efforts of our young *protégée* to redeem it from its mediocrity. She has too little scope, you see, in an *ingénue*'s role.

"I believe that the failure of *Le Chevalier Malcontent*– my failure–has shaken the confidence of the whole company a little, and Lillette is no exception. Had *Le Chevalier* been a success, she would doubtless have stored up the confidence needed to tackle a more challenging and rewarding role, but as things are, she is a trifle fragile. You are the one man who can repair her fragility: the man who can pay her the greatest compliment in the world, merely by expressing his belief in her. She adores you, as you know. It would mean so much to her. Will you help me to sustain and protect her progress toward the glorious destiny of stardom? Will you tell her that within a month–no, three weeks–she will *know*, beyond the shadow of a doubt, that I have given her the means to shine as brightly in the theatrical firmament as any star of the 19th and 20th centuries: that I have given her the means to become a living legend?"

"Three weeks, you say," the Comte observed. "A moment ago, Monsieur Moineaux, you were speaking of three days."

"Three days to obtain the copies of the script, provided that Lavinière is not overloaded with work, and a further three weeks to prepare the performances. When we read a play–I say 'we' because I count you as expert a reader as myself–we may find a seed that holds the potential of a mighty tree, but it is not until we can see the piece acted out that we glimpse the bole and the crown, and obtain preliminary estimates of its eventual height and the luxury of its boughs. In three weeks, Comte–when the new play's opening is but a few days away, Lillette will know as well as you or I what a future she has."

"May I know the title of the play?" the Comte asked.

"I may change the title," Moineaux countered.

"May I know the author's name?"

"No one, as yet, would recognize the author's name," Moineaux told him, adding for good measure: "which is, at any rate, a pseudonym. One day, though, it will be graven upon the face of posterity, along with the names of those who brought it into the light. I shall be proud to be in that company, Monsieur le Comte, although my name will be a mere footnote compared to the name of Lillette Fevret."

"You have a nice turn of phrase, Monsieur Moineaux," the Comte observed, his voice delicately tinted with contempt. "Perhaps you are a playwright yourself–under a pseudonym, of course?"

In his capacity as an actor-manager Moineaux had, of course, rewritten more plays than any modern author had written, sometimes so extensively that their originators could hardly recognize their work, but he had never considered himself a mere writer, he was so much more than that. He was a true creator, charged with bringing living dramatic order out of chaotic verbal sketches. He did not take offense at the

Comte's remark, though, even secretly. He liked to consider himself a generous and forgiving man as well as a diplomat.

"We are all playwrights, in the truest sense of the word, Monsieur le Comte," he said. "We are all collaborators in the great endeavor that is the theater. We all have our parts to play within the great seamless whole, the inviolable unity. Tell me that you are with me, sire, I beg of you. What a great adventure we shall have! What a triumph shall be ours! Tell me, please, that you will prevail upon your *protégée* to take this part."

The Comte de Farineux looked the actor-manager squarely in the eye, and said: "We are no longer young men, Monsieur Moineaux. I was famous once, just as you were, but we are very near to being forgotten now. Lillette has her whole adult life in front of her, but you and I have little to look forward to but our dotage. We know what we have to lose, and that we are bound to lose it in the end. We have a similar sense of urgency, and a similar consciousness of the extent to which our fates have recently been bound together by our darling Lillette. I will grant you your three weeks, Monsieur Moineaux, because I know, as you do, how precious time is to men of our antiquity. Show me what you can do, Monsieur Moineaux—but I beg you not to disappoint me. Age has evidently mellowed you, but it has not treated me as kindly. I had my fill of disappointment long ago, and I no longer react well to such sensations."

Moineaux bowed deeply. "You do yourself a disservice, sire, in deprecating your own eloquence. It would have been within your compass to be a great writer as well as a great actor, had destiny not marked you out for a more glorious vocation. I thank you from the bottom of my heart."

By the time he had descended the steps of the *perron* leading down from the Comte's house to the street, the once-great Stéphane Moineaux was sweating like a *jeune premier* about to take the stage in his first major role, and his heart was hammering. He had cleared the second hurdle that malevolent happenstance had set in his path, but that had only brought him back to the point from which he had started the night before. He was still in want of a play, and his lack was more desperate than ever.

In gaining a stay of execution from the Comte, Moineaux had spelled out his need more clearly than before. He had specified a deadline, and had stated in so many words that he needed a work of outstanding quality. That had always been his need, but while he had only felt it vaguely it had not seemed so intimidating. Now he knew the exact depth of his predicament. It was as well to confront the fact squarely, he supposed, but now that he was staring his fate in the face he could see all too easily how unpromising his situation was.

He needed a stroke of good luck so outrageous in its proportions as almost to constitute a miracle.

Moineaux walked to the cab-stand in the Rue Serpente and hired a battered *fiacre* whose horse ought to have been put out to grass or turned into glue five years before. He gave the morose driver Monsieur Lavinière's address on the Quai des Orfèvres.

The carriage set off at a trot so feeble that Moineaux could probably have outsprinted it to the bank of the Seine– but he was painfully aware of the fact that he could no longer have outstayed it, even as far the Pont-Neuf.

4

By the time Moineaux got down from the *fiacre* on to the cobblestones of the Quai, he was firmly decided that he must take a strong line with Lavinière. If the copyist could not be seduced into parting with useful information, then he must be bullied into it, for there was no way that Moineaux could come up with a sufficient bribe.

When he was shown into Lavinière's private office by the copy-shop manager's assistant and asked to wait,

Moineaux was initially pleased. It gave him an opportunity to riffle through the papers on the desk, reading Lavinière's correspondence and scanning his work-lists. When the interval extended far beyond the time required for such rapid espionage, however, the actor became irritated. To keep a person of his status waiting was more than a personal insult; it was an insult to the sacred hierarchy of the theatrical profession.

When Monsieur Lavinière finally consented to appear, he was, admittedly, exceedingly apologetic. He explained that the volume and urgency of his commissioned work, and the necessity of training several new typists, had not given him a moment's rest since daybreak. Moineaux dutifully concealed his annoyance, not only accepting the apology gracefully but offering one of his own for having descended upon his old friend without prior warning.

"I'm delighted that business is booming, my dear fellow," the actor-manager proclaimed. "We're living in exciting times in the world of the theater. So much new work, so many new directions! And you, old friend, are at the very heart of it, with your finger on the pulse of its progress. You not only read everything, but you read everything before anyone else sees it. Before any play is produced, let alone printed, your legion of typists produce the scripts from which the actors learn their lines–the raw material of their performances. What a privileged position you occupy! How many years has it been since I first brought a script to you for copying? It was 1873, I think–the spring. It was *Gouttes de Sang*, I believe–not my finest production, by any means but one I'll always remember fondly. Twenty-six years! Half a lifetime!"

"The present system," Lavinière informed him, "is that my clients leave scripts to be copied with my assistant. It's no longer possible for me to see all comers personally."

"But old acquaintances–old friends–are not *all comers!*" Moineaux protested. "You're working too hard, my dear fellow. You need a break."

"Where's the script?" Lavinière asked, brutally. "How many copies, and when do you need them?"

As he pronounced the final sentence, Lavinière's ruddy features creased into a frown. The copyist's eyes had roamed hither and yon, and found no evidence of any manuscript.

Moineaux had never known anyone, apart from Lavinière, whose frown extended all the way from his brow to his chin–but he had never known another man whose wrinkles were quite as mazy as Lavinière's. The copyist was only a year or two older than Moineaux–perhaps the same age as the Comte de Farineux– but the anxieties of life had made a far deeper impression on his flesh.

"I do not have the script with me, at present," Moineaux admitted. "The author is making final corrections–you know what niggardly perfectionists these writers can be, even though they know that half their words will be discarded in the course of rehearsals and the other half expanded by way of compensation. I called in because I knew that you were busy, in order to reserve time in your schedule in advance of the submission. When the author consents to let go of his nursling, I shall need it copied in a hurry–time is if the essence."

"Reserve time in advance?" Lavinière queried. "I don't do that, Monsieur Moineaux. Scripts are copied strictly in order of their submission. That's the way it's always been, and the way it has to be. It's the only fair way to do business."

"It's not so long ago that people were unable to book theater seats in advance–except for the rich, who could rent boxes in perpetuity," Moineaux observed, "but we move with the times, do we not? Even the humblest patron can now reserve his seat a week or a month ahead of time, in order that he might plan his social calendar as carefully as a Comte or a Duc. You seem fractious, old friend, and overtired, although it's not yet three o'clock. I'm a busy man myself, as you know, and we've a performance to put on at the Tragicomique tonight, but I'd be a poor friend if I didn't offer to buy you a glass of wine, or even an early dinner–being an *habitué* of the theatrical *monde*, of course, you'll be well used to theatrical meal-times. I must insist–it's for your own good. Come with me, and we'll spare a little time from our hectic schedules to talk about old times."

"I can't," Lavinière said–and said no more.

Moineaux was amazed and appalled. To refuse such a kind invitation was bad enough–it was tantamount to treason against etiquette as well as the sacred bond of amity–but to refuse it so bluntly, without the least hint of apology or excuse, was quite unforgivable. "My dear Lavinière," he said, solicitously, "I believe you're making yourself ill with all this rushing around. I don't trust physicians, as you know, but I trust my common sense, and my advice in such matters is never wrong. I prescribe an immediate respite, and a leisurely bite to eat, with good conversation. There's no question of inability; it's imperative, and that's all there is to it. Pick up your hat, and we'll go."

"I have too much to do, Monsieur Moineaux," the copyist stated, flatly. The maze of his wrinkles had become quite insoluble. "You're very welcome to bring your script when it's ready, and I promise you that my typists will get to work on it as soon as it reaches the top of the heap, but I really don't have time to spare for idle chitchat."

Stéphane Moineaux had been a great actor in his day, and he still prided himself on being utterly unflustered by anything that happened on a stage. When his fellow actors missed their cues, or dried up, or lost their places and produced the wrong lines, he was always ready to improvise repairs, but the suggestion that his conversation was *idle chitchat* left him speechless. He stared at the copyist in frank astonishment.

Instead of being overcome by shame and contrition, however, Monsieur Lavinière actually turned to leave the room, saying: "My assistant will show you out. Good day to you, Monsieur Moineaux."

For several months, Moineaux had been living with the knowledge that his career, and his world, might come to an ignominious end sooner rather than later. Thus far, his only response to this anxiety and expectation had been one of bold defiance. The threat of bankruptcy had called forth a fervent determination to fight to the last ditch, no matter how much stage blood he had to shed in the process. Now, he felt that the world might already have reached its terminus, and that the ultimate desolation might already be setting in. It seemed, suddenly, that the day of judgement had arrived–and that the angel armed with the last trump was an antique copyist whose only distinguishing feature was the bizarre quality of his frown.

The world had evidently gone mad, by way of preparation for its destruction.

Moineaux was tempted to plead with the copyist for a moment more of his seemingly-valuable time. He was even tempted to say: "Do you realize who you're talking to?"

Alas, the once-great actor knew that Lavinière knew full well who he was talking to–and that was the problem. Lavinière knew exactly what his old friend wanted from him, and why. Unlike Paul Damas and the Comte de Farineux, he was not willing to allow himself to be talked into giving Moineaux what he needed, and might perish without. Whatever information he had, he was no longer willing to share it with the manager of the Théâtre Tragicomique. Lavinière the copyist had made up his mind that Stéphane Moineaux was a has-been, a man without a future.

What a brutal age we live in! Moineaux thought, as Lavinière's assistant did indeed usher him out on to the street. *Friendship is dead, loyalty extinct, good faith obliterated.*

Even though the river traffic had dwindled sharply in the last decade, the Quai des Orfèvres was abuzz with activity. The footpath was crowded with pedestrians; the business establishments–which were much more various now than they had been in 1873, when Lavinière's shop had seemed a bizarre adventure–were still at the peak of their daily activity despite the relative lateness of the hour. The carriages making their way along the Quai formed a seemingly-endless train–except for one that was parked just outside Lavinière's door.

Moineaux, choked with emotion, lurched away from the door like a shipwrecked sailor cast away on some barren strand–a part still well within his compass on stage, but which seemed direly uncomfortable in reality. He might have fallen down had there not been a newly-erected lamp-post outside Lavinière's door, on which he was able to lean for a few moments.

I'll be better off out of such an unkind world, Moineaux said to himself, letting his train of thought run on, impelled by the momentum of his bitterness. *I ought no longer to have any desire to belong to such an ungrateful society. I have given my all to my art and my audience, and have been well and truly damned for taking the trouble. If this is now the way of things on Earth, even in Paris, then I shall be better off in the grave, or in the fires of Hell.*

When the momentary shock had passed, however, Moineaux put his own hat back on his head, and pulled himself together. Not caring that he was speaking aloud to himself in a crowded street, he said: "There must be someone else who can tell me what I need to know. I shall drop in on the offices of the *Mercure* and see Vallette. He's worth ten of Lavinière, in any case... and his wife is a melodramatist of some repute. He will treat me politely, and he will tell me where I can find a play."

He looked up at the coachman seated on the platform of the carriage that was parked outside Monsieur Lavinière's establishment, although he had known at first glance that it was not for hire. It was a smart *coupé* drawn by two jet black horses, which would not have looked out of place at Longchamp. The coachman looked down at Moineaux with the insolent contempt that servants sometimes manifest for those among their betters who do not seem to have the power to hurt them, but the blackguard did not go so far as to make any suggestive gesture with his whip.

Moineaux thought better of asking whether there was any possibility of obtaining a lift as far as Alfred Vallette's office. He did not think he could bear a curt refusal. He was about to go off on foot when the copyist's door opened again. A small, stout man wearing a valet's uniform came out, carrying a substantial stack of acting scripts.

The small man hurried to the door of the *coupé*, which had obviously been waiting to collect him. His uniform was clean and relatively new, but the garments had something about them that was suggestive of Breton barbarism; his master was obviously not a Parisian.

Moineaux made a supreme effort, drew himself up to his full height in order to look down imperiously upon the valet, and said: "To which theater are you taking those scripts, my good man?"

"To the Grand Guignol, Monsieur," was the polite reply.

"Ah yes," said Moineaux. "Monsieur Méténier's latest commission, no doubt–another adaptation of Poe, perhaps... or some new *conte cruel* by my good friend Monsieur Level."

"No, Monsieur," the small man said, frowning slightly because Moineaux was blocking the carriage door–and because he could not do anything about it, given the evident difference in their respective social positions. "My master is a new playwright, who hopes to persuade Monsieur Méténier to stage his work. He has paid for copies to be made in order to save the theater some expense–and to have an adequate supply of samples, in case he has to show it to other potential producers."

This statement generated a torrent of mixed emotions in Stéphane Moineaux's desperate heart. Amateur playwrights who had their work copied in advance of receiving a commission were almost invariably *rentiers* possessed of abundant monetary means but utterly devoid of talent. There was no more than one chance in a thousand that the script would be worth reading–but that was one more chance than Moineaux could lay his hands on, at present, by groping in any other direction.

The actor-manager added his most commanding expression to his carefully-poised pose, and said: "Monsieur, I am Stéphane Moineaux, tragedian and owner of the Théâtre

Tragicomique. Monsieur Méténier is my great friend and esteemed colleague, and he told me only yesterday that he will not be able to accept any new plays until November, at the earliest. It is possible, however, that I might be able to put in a word on your master's behalf, if were to consider the cause sufficiently worthy. If you would care to take me to see your master, and let me read his play *en route*, I shall be glad to consider the possibility with all due care. It is conceivable that I might be able to save your master a good deal of time–and I'm sure that his time is very precious to him."

The valet was obviously very reluctant to agree to this proposition, but Moineaux was still blocking the carriage door and had no intention of moving. In the end, the little man said: "I suppose it would do no harm, Monsieur, given that you are a theater-owner, if you were to look at one of the scripts. Perhaps the master will see you, given the eminence of your position."

Moineaux climbed up into the carriage with alacrity, and seated himself with his back to the coachman. He thrust out a hand, and the little man allowed him to take the topmost copy from the pile of scripts before placing the remainder carefully on the other seat."

As the carriage drew off, Moineaux bit his lip, for the title-page of the script read: *Le Nouveau Faust* by Simon de Keramour. The playwright's name was instantly recognizable as a pseudonym, and Moineaux knew only too well that if there was one story in the world that had been done to literary death, it was the legend of Faust. No tale on Earth could possibly have survived being chosen as the subject of so many operas.

"I'm doomed, and damned to destitution," Moineaux muttered, inaudibly. Then, in a much louder and clearer voice, he said: "This is surely destiny, my friend. Your master and I will doubtless have a great deal to discuss. Let's be off, while I give my full attention to my reading." In fact, the *coupé* had already moved off, but Moineaux thought it worth cultivating the impression that he was in a position to give orders.

He told himself, sternly, that there was always room in the theater for a new version of *Faust*, and always scope for a truly great actor to bring out the best in Mephistopheles. He reminded himself, too, that there had been many a *Faust* that had made as much of the part of Marguerite as that of the scholar-conjuror and his demon, and that Lillette Fevret might thrive in such a role.

He was not entirely convinced by his own rhetoric, but he turned to the list of *dramatis personae* with a small seed of hope in his heart, and he scanned it rapidly.

5

Moineaux learned at a glance that Monsieur de Kera-mour's Faust was forenamed Jean, because he was a French-man of relatively recent antiquity rather than a 17th-century German. Jean Faust was identified by the notes accompanying the name as a man of science and philosopher of progress, contemporary with Antoine Lavoisier, the Chevalier de Lamarck and the Marquis de Condorcet, who had reached the age of 60 at the time of the play's first act, set in the year 1804.

The notes specified that two contrasting actors—one young and one mature—would be required to play the part of Jean Faust, because one aspect of his particular diabolical bargain involved his rejuvenation, which was achieved by his trading bodies with Mephistopheles, here initially manifest as a virile youth. The same two actors would, of course, be required to play Mephistopheles in the complementary phases of the play.

Stéphane Moineaux had played both Faust and Mephistopheles in his time, but never in the course of the same performance. Paul Damas had never played either, but would doubtless find the prospect of such a dual role intriguing.

"So far, so good," he murmured, still trying to evoke the power of positive thinking. The actor-manager's eye traveled swiftly down the page, conscious of the fact that his most urgent need was a suitable role for Lillette Fevret. His spirits rose as he saw that the next name included in the cast-list was also part of a double role.

Jean Faust was not young enough, at the beginning of the play, to have a female counterpart symbolic of the attractions of marriage and domesticity, but there was nevertheless a Marguerite on the list: a young pupil, fired with post-Revolutionary ambition. The notes commented that she was avid to acquire Faust's knowledge and wisdom, in order that she might liberate herself from the traditional condition of womankind and become a sort of *bourgeois* Emilie du Châtelet: a mistress of Newtonian Enlightenment and Voltairean skepticism. The actress playing this role was also required to play a beautiful courtesan–expressly identified as a personification of Lust–in opposition to the rejuvenated Faust.

There's a reasonable chance, Moineaux thought, *that I can persuade the Comte that this is, indeed, the challenging and potentially-rewarding role I described to him... always provided that the script itself lives up to the promise of its cast.*

He noted, *en passant*, that there was yet another double role in the list. The actress playing Marguerite's mother, ardently desirous of forcing her daughter into conventional marriage and placid domesticity, had also to play the mother of the courtesan, who was equally desirous of promoting her own daughter's more lurid, but equally conventional, career. This exercise in comparison and contrast, Moineaux supposed, might require just enough flair, and have enough inherent interest in it, to take the edge off Marianne Jonquille's inevitable resistance to the idea of playing a maternal role in association with a much younger female lead.

Moineaux's hand trembled slightly as he turned the pages, and his practiced eyes began to skim through Act One, Scene One. He was soon engrossed–so engrossed, in fact, that he did not immediately notice when the *coupé* pulled up.

When he did realize that the journey was ended, he pulled out his pocket-watch, having lost track of the time.

The watch's hands indicated 3:30. He was due on stage at 7:30, and had to be back at the theater by seven, at the latest, in order to put on his make-up. He looked out of the carriage window to see where they were, in order that he could estimate how long it would take to get back to the Tragicomique.

Somewhat to his surprise—for he had lived in Paris for nearly half a century—Moineaux did not recognize the neighborhood in which the *coupé* had come to a halt. The street was narrow and the houses ancient; he could easily have believed that he was back in the old Paris of his youth, before Baron Haussmann had wrought his magical transformation—but there were a dozen such enclaves scattered around the various *arrondissements*, like stagnant ponds, and he was not familiar with all of them.

The valet had already descended to the footpath and lowered the footplate for Moineaux's convenience. When Moineaux had got out, the servant stepped back up again to retrieve the pile of scripts before scurrying to the main door of an edifice that could not have been built any later than 1700, and had not been much repaired in the interim. Because the street was so narrow and the houses were so tall, the Sun was entirely obscured and the whole terrace was becalmed in deep shadow. Many of the street's windows were shuttered despite the hour, including those in the house whose bell the valet had rung.

When another servant came in response to the ring and stood aside to let him in, Moineaux found himself entering a corridor that was almost pitch-dark even before the door was closed behind him.

"This way, Monsieur," said a whispering voice, which sounded strangely sinister in the gloom. A hand took his arm and drew him forwards, until the voice said: "Be careful of the stairs, Monsieur."

Despite the warning, Moineaux stumbled awkwardly on the first step of an ascending staircase. "Why the Devil don't you light a candle, if you have no gaslamps?" he asked.

"There is a candle alight in the master's study," the whispering voice answered. "Please be patient, Monsieur Moineaux."

With the aid of his guide, the actor-manager reached the top of the stair without further mishap, and moved along another corridor. He scraped his thigh on a side-table and caught his toe in a rucked-up rug, but contrived to stay on his feet until he was asked to wait.

A door opened to his left, but Moineaux had no time to take stock of the room within before the valet had disappeared and pushed the door to behind him.

A whispered conversation began behind the door, but the voices were so soft that Moineaux could only make out a few fragmentary words. The exchange went on for more than three minutes before the door was opened wide again.

"My master will see you, Monsieur Moineaux," the valet said. "I must ask you to speak quietly, for his ears are as sensitive as his eyes."

Moineaux went into the candlelit room, leaving the valet to close the door behind him.

The walls of the study were entirely lined with tightly-stuffed bookshelves, save for the doorway, the capacious fireplace and two tall but rather narrow windows, both of which were shuttered without. There was a huge desk in the center of the room, with two miniature filing-cabinets mounted to either side of the writing-pad and two candlesticks positioned in front of the filing-cabinets. Each candlestick contained a lighted candle that had burned down almost to a stub. The inkwell was unusually ornate, carved into the semblance of a skull. All the pens in the rack had steel nibs, but some of them had wooden shafts carved to resemble quills.

A leather-upholstered armchair was drawn up in front of the desk, but it had been pushed back at an angle while its former occupant got up to fetch its twin from a book-lined corner. Moineaux's avid gaze scanned the bookshelves; most were packed with yellow paperbacks, but there were a few shelves of leather-bound tomes that must have been at least fifty years old, and there were scattered volumes that had been more durably bound. The piles on the floor included a number of quarto volumes, mostly bound in dingy blue cloth. The carpet on which they rested was patterned in red and blue, but dust obscured the outlines of the pattern.

The man who brought a second armchair to the desk was tall and slender, apparently between 20 and 30 years of age, with skin so pale that he might almost have been an albino, although his eyes were blue rather than pink and his hair was blonde rather than white. He was not an unhandsome man, but there was a strange mournfulness in the arrangement of his features, which refused to be banished by the smile with which he favored his visitor.

"It's an honor to make your acquaintance, Monsieur Moineaux," the playwright said, as he positioned the second armchair close to his own and invited his visitor to sit. "I know your reputation, of course, although I regret that I have never had the opportunity to see you perform. I have not been long in Paris. I am Simon de Keramour, as you presumably know." As he spoke the last few words, the pale man gestured towards the script that Moineaux was holding in his hand, then added: "Would you like a glass of wine?"

Moineaux was slightly nonplussed, being still convinced that "Simon de Keramour" was a pseudonym, and by the fact that his host's accent was quite indefinable as to its origin. He accepted the offer of a glass of wine as he sat down, and watched his host pour from a bottle of burgundy that already stood open on the desk, beside the writing pad. It proved to be a very tolerable Pinot Noir.

"To judge by your name and your valet's clothing," Moineaux said, "you are presumably a Breton. I knew your late compatriot, Monsieur Paul Féval, and have had the honor of acting in several of his plays. My Lagardère was quite famous at one time–but you must have been a child then."

"Monsieur Féval was born in Rennes, I believe," de Keramour said. "My own family is from Ploemeur, although we have not lived there for several generations. I am familiar with Monsieur Féval's novels, but not, alas, his dramatic works. My valet tells me that you seemed to like my play, and were deeply absorbed in it all the way from the Quai des Orfèvres."

"I do like it," Moineaux told him. "It lacks polish, but I think there is every evidence, so far as I have read, that it might easily be refined by a skilful and experienced director, and brought to life by the right cast."

"I intend to offer it to Monsieur Méténier," the playwright said. "His establishment seems to be very popular just now."

"So popular, alas," Moineaux said, "that it would not be easy for an untried writer like yourself to interest him in a project unless you had an influential advocate. I've skimmed through the first two acts, however, and I believe that Monsieur Méténier could be persuaded to look at it if it came to him with my recommendation. He would then hand it over to one of his contracted writers for revision without delay. It will probably have to be abridged to meet his exacting requirements, and Monsieur Méténier will doubtless want to replace the dialogue in Act Two that discusses theories of evolution, revolution, temptation and progress with something less challenging, perhaps to reinforce the comedy relief. It is rumored that some of the leading actors in his company are due to be rested, due to exhaustion, and he might think your play a suitable opportunity to give his younger players an outing—perhaps as early as in August, which is traditionally a quiet season in the theater."

"I do not want my play to be handed over to a contract writer for revision," Simon de Keramour said, very softly. "I could not tolerate any undue interference with the dialogue you mention, which is the very heart of the play—and I would not care for my work to be performed by secondary members of a company in a quiet season."

43

"It would not be ideal, of course," Moineaux said, taking a sip from his glass before shrugging his shoulders expressively. "But what can one do? Monsieur Méténier is a thoroughly modern director, and he works in a thoroughly modern way. Things went differently in my heyday, but times move on. Monsieur Méténier done not have the respect for writers that directors used to have; he regards his business as a purely commercial enterprise, and the plays he puts on as commercial products in need of standardization. He is a great believer in what he calls *scientific management*."

"Scientific management?" the playwright echoed, seemingly aghast. "In the theater?"

"It is not my philosophy, I must admit," Moineaux said. "But who am I to criticize Monsieur Méténier? His productions are, as you say, very popular. He is a fine man and a very successful one. He respects my opinion as an actor and director despite the differences in our outlook. I think I might be able to persuade him to take the risk of putting his leading actors into your play—perhaps as early as next February, if you were willing to compromise on the matter of rewriting. He would not assign the job of rewriting to any mere hack, you understand; Monsieur Level is a fine craftsman, if one cares for that sort of work, and the rumor that he secretly passes some of his many commissions to his wife for lack of time is not to be trusted. Paris is a den of vipers, you know, when it comes to jealous gossip. One does what one can to rise above it."

Simon de Keramour's blue eyes seemed strange in the dim light, perhaps because the pupils—which ought to have been widely dilated—were mere pin-pricks in the center of oceanic irises. They were fixed on Moineaux with remarkable intensity.

"What you say is, I confess, more than slightly distressing," the playwright admitted. "I am not very familiar with the customs and habits of the Parisian theater, and I had not realized that Monsieur Méténier operated his establishment in that way. I have only been to the Grand Guignol once; I prefer the

Opéra-Comique and the Ambigu-Comique for lighter material, but I thought that I might be aiming too high were I to take my script to one or other of those companies. Do you have any influence with their managers, perhaps?"

"Oh yes," Moineaux said, airily. "Everyone in the world of the theater knows me. The younger men dare to consider me a little outdated, but they respect my vast experience. The Ambigu might offer the better opportunity, although you might have to be a little more patient. The manager there has obligations that extend at least until next April, and he might not be able to stage your play until September 1900. On the other hand, that would give you plenty of time to rework it according to his instructions. He's a hard taskmaster, but at least he refuses to hire contract men to rewrite plays. How will authors ever learn, he says, if they do not do the work themselves? He always issues very abundant notes. He might be slightly more tolerant of the dialogue in Act Two, provided that it can be accommodated to suit his taste in political satire."

"And that," Simon de Kéramour said, bleakly, "is what you would consider to be the better opportunity?"

Moineaux shrugged again. "It is the way things are done nowadays," he said. "There are very few of us left who cleave to the old ways. What a pleasure it was to work with men like Monsieur Féval! We once put a play on within a fortnight of his putting the final touches to the script. It went straight into rehearsal; the scene-painters got to work; posters were plastered all over Paris virtually overnight–and it was a great success! What I wouldn't give to be able to embark upon that sort of adventure nowadays! But I'm getting old, alas, and it requires a worthy challenge to rouse me to such extraordinary efforts. It took a full three months to get *Le Chevalier Malcontent* ready, and I regret to confess that it's hardly bringing in enough money to keep the theater open. It's a good play, mind, with fine performances from Monsieur Damas and Mademoiselle Fevret. Perhaps I should have taken a leaf out of Monsieur Méténier's book and tightened it up a little more, but I hate to interfere with the basic thrust of a writer's work—it seems so disrespectful. Given time, I think the audiences might pick up. Word of mouth is the best publicity, after all, and although the Guignol's name is on the lips of the larger public just now, there's always a more discerning audience who talk more seriously about the important and enduring dramatic qualities. Do you know the Comte de Farineux, by any chance?"

"I recognize the name," the playwright said, "but I have never met the man. My name retains a hint of ancient aristocracy, but it is Breton aristocracy rather than French, and my family had moved down the social scale long before the Revolution of 1789. I am a scholar of sorts, and am acquainted with a number of aristocratic antiquarians, but I do not move in the same social circles as the military heroes of the Second Empire."

"He has become a great aficionado of the theater since he replaced his sword in his scabbard for good," Moineaux said. "He is the sort of man I mean when I speak of a more discerning audience. I am honored to have him as a regular in the green room at the Tragicomique, and always glad to see him in his box. He's very smitten with Mademoiselle Fevret, and she admires him tremendously. He thinks her part in *Le Chevalier Malcontent* quite the best thing she has done, and is deeply disappointed with its poor reception. He's doing his best to talk it up in the *salons*, though, and his efforts might bear fruit in time. The alternative, which would be to close it early, is the kind of bleak prospect that I never confront without sadness."

"Are you considering that alternative?" de Keramour asked.

"A man in my position must always be considering every possibility," Moineaux replied, with a deep sigh. "Life was so much easier in the carefree days when I was merely an actor, able to give myself entirely to my role. I still do, of course, when I'm on stage—but as soon as the curtain comes down, the burdens of management and ownership descend upon me like one of Monsieur Baudelaire's chimeras. Each man has his own, the poet says, and mine is the responsibility of caring for the future of my flock–by which I mean my company."

Moineaux paused to take another sip of wine.

Simon de Keramour did not pick up the thread of the conversation immediately; his blue eyes were staring into infinity, as if searching for something. Moineaux did not permit the ghost of a smile to appear on his lips, but he congratulated himself inwardly. The fish was hooked.

He was not sure, as yet, that the fish would actually reward the skill of his angling, but with nothing else to set on his table he had to play the game to win. One way or another, he felt, *Le Nouveau Faust* would probably have to settle his fate, even though he had not yet read enough of Act Three to know whether Jean Faust would be damned at the end or not.

6

"It's really for the sake of my players that I keep the Tragicomique going," Moineaux went on, as Simon de Keramour remained lost in thought. "I sometimes think that I'd as soon be rid of the responsibility. I dream of going back to the Gambardi or the Gymnase, merely as a player in a company, forgetting commerce and devoting myself entirely to art–but an actor-manager is a father with a huge family, who cannot ever think of himself."

He took out his watch, ostentatiously, and looked at the hands. "Time marches on," he said. "I'm due on stage at 7:30, and I have a thousand things to do before I can even begin to apply my make-up. I must go–but you have my solemn promise that I will talk to Monsieur Méténier for you, and the manager at the Ambigu too, when I have the chance. Depend on me, Monsieur de Keramour; it may take time, but your play will be produced eventually–and it will be the first of many, I'm sure."

Moineaux stood up, as if to go to the door, but Simon de Keramour was quick to lean forward and pour him another glass of wine.

"Don't go just yet," the playwright said. "I'll ask my coachman to drive you back in a little while. My team is excellent, and although the fellow was schooled on rural roads, he's taken to the crowded streets of Paris like a duck to water. You don't know what a privilege it is for me to talk to a man with such vast theatrical experience as yourself. I'm quite naive in these matters, for all my reading and my determination to write for the stage. I'm fascinated to have an insight into the mind and work of a distinguished actor-manager. What would you do if you were forced to close your present production early? Wouldn't that leave an awkward hole in your program?"

"Yes it would," Moineaux agreed, "but hard decisions sometimes have to be taken, and one has to be ready to improvise. We have a number of plays in our repertoire, of course, and the easiest option would be to bring back one that we staged last year or the year before. There's always room for a revival by popular demand–not that it would actually be by popular demand, strictly speaking, but one has to represent forced moves in the best possible light."

"Couldn't you put on a new play?"

"That would be more difficult. Even if I had the right play under contract, it would take much longer to memorize and rehearse it, let alone to smooth the dialogue and hone the action scenes to the require precision of movement. One can't perfect the flow of a play without completed sets, and one often has to refine and remold the sets to accommodate the evolution of its direction. In the old days, of course, with everyone pulling together and working flat out... but that was then, and this is now. The old days are gone, alas."

"But why?" de Keramour asked. "What was possible then is surely possible now. What wouldn't you give, you said only a few minutes ago, to embark on such an adventure? Why not?"

Moineaux allowed his expression to become rapt with anticipation, and then become clouded again. "Ah!" he sighed. "You paint an enticing picture, Monsieur de Keramour. You Bretons have so much romance in your soul. I believe Monsieur Féval would have said exactly the same, God bless him— and he'd have thrown himself into the venture like one of his own heroes. If I had a man like him beside me..." He trailed off, with a tantalizing expertise born of 40 years' experience, man and boy.

"You make it sound a very attractive proposition," de Keramour observed.

"Do I?" Moineaux asked, wondering exactly how far he could go without overplaying his hand. "I shouldn't, you know. It's pure self-indulgence. No actor-manager in Paris would contemplate such a thing nowadays. Anyway, it's out of the question. I have no new play to put on in *Le Chevalier*'s place, even if I had time to prepare it. If I'm forced to close it, I shall have to use something from the company's repertoire."

"Would you be prepared to consider *my* play?" the author asked, finally biting the bullet.

Moineaux paused, as if for serious thought, holding a mouthful of wine on his palate so that he could savor the taste—but he did not pause long before gulping it down. "Would you be prepared to offer me your play, Monsieur de Keramour?" he said. "The Tragicomique has a more capacious auditorium than the Grand Guignol, but we're hardly as fashionable—and the Ambigu has the advantage on both counts. All I could offer you by way of compensation is an excellent cast. Paul Damas and Lillette Fevret would be pleased to be offered the complex and challenging parts that your play demands, and the Comte would be delighted to think that his *protégée* was surrendering an excellent role in order to take an outstanding one. Do you think I would be quite right for your Faust-turned-Mephistopheles, though? I might be a little too old."

"It would be an honor," Simon de Keramour said, responding to his cue like a seasoned performer, "to have an actor of your stature take one of the leading roles in my play. I trust your judgement implicitly with respect to the talents of the junior members of your company. What attracts me most about the possibility of your producing my play is however, the lack of delay. I'm eager to see it staged, and the possibility of opening it in June is an exciting one. Would you be willing to do that?"

"I haven't finished reading the play, as yet," Moineaux remarked, "but if Act Three lives up to the promise of Acts One and Two, I dare say that I would... and if all went well, I dare say that I could."

"If you're prepared to consider the possibility, I would do everything I can to help," the playwright assured him. "I am not Monsieur Féval, of course, but..."

"But you are a fine writer," Moineaux put in, deftly completing the sentence, "and a true gentleman of the theater. Do you know, Monsieur de Keramour, ever since I sat down and took a sip of your excellent wine, I have had the strangest feeling that you and I were destined to meet."

"Perhaps we were, Monsieur Moineaux," the playwright agreed.

"I may be getting old," Moineaux continued, "but I'm not too old to relish an adventure. To put on your play would be a risk–but what is life but an infinite series of risks, which cry out to be taken boldly? If fate might be on our side, nothing is impossible. I would be failing in my responsibility, of course, if I didn't read your play more carefully, all the way through to the end, but I'm confident that my first impression will not be overturned. If I finish it in bed tonight, I would be able to have a contract drawn up and ready for signature by tomorrow morning, if you were to call at the theater at 11 a.m... Yes, I am now persuaded! *Le Chevalier Malcontent* will close early, and it will be replaced by *Le Nouveau Faust*!" He raised his glass, in which he had carefully preserved one last mouthful of Pinot Noir. "A toast, my new friend, to our future relationship! We shall be colleagues, allies and partners. Together, we shall do great things!"

Simon de Keramour winced visibly, and Moineaux realized that he had raised his voice in his excitement—but the playwright made no complaint, and raised his own glass to drink to the bargain they had made. In the flickering light of the dying candles, the wine in their glasses took on a particular red hue that Moineaux had never seen before, as pure and bright as a martyr's blood in one of Rochegrosse's gaudier canvases.

"I must, of course, make certain conditions," the playwright said, as the two men replaced their empty glasses on the desk-top.

Moineaux's heart skipped a beat. "What do you mean?" he asked.

"Apart from the opportunity to have it produced without too long a delay," Simon de Keramour told him, "I am enthused by the prospect of my play being produced as I wrote it, with its heart and soul intact, rather than being rewritten by some hired hack or in accordance with strict instructions. The latter consideration is, in fact, the more important of the two."

"Plays always evolve in rehearsal," Moineaux told him. "Their scripts must be responsive to the lessons that emerge from the players' interpretation of the words. Just as the characters' movements must be adapted to the requirements of the set, so their speeches must be adapted to the requirements of the cast and direction."

"I do not mind making modifications that seem to me to be required," the playwright said, "and I am certainly willing to listen to your expert advice, but I feel obliged to warn you that if modifications were to be forced upon me, against my judgement, then I would rather take the play elsewhere and wait for a more sympathetic director. I fear that I must insist on that right being written into the contract."

"I understand your anxiety," Moineaux said, feeling now that he was the fish on the hook, and Simon de Keramour the skilful angler. "You must understand, though, that I have 40 years of experience in the theater. I am always respectful of an author's intentions, and my first priority is always to bring his ideas to life as faithfully as is humanly possible, but it is sometimes the case that lines which sound very effective in the privacy of a writer's mind do not sound as well when they are voiced. The texts of classic dramas acquire a quality of sacredness, but their perfection is often the result of intensive reworking in their early performances; every script needs to be put to the proof, my friend, and every author needs to be flexible."

"I assure you that I am not an unreasonable man," Simon de Keramour said, insistently. "If you can persuade me by reasonable argument that something in my play needs to be changed, then I will allow the change–but I must retain the right to withdraw the play rather than suffer changes of which I do not approve."

"Of course you must," Moineaux replied, in a placatory tone. "I shall always defend an author's right to resist abuse. We shall work together harmoniously, I feel sure. You have my solemn promise that I will consult you carefully with regard to any changes that seem to me to be essential, and that you will always have the final word."

"And that will be written in the contract, will it not?" the playwright persisted.

"If you so wish," the actor-manager conceded.

Providence has gifted me one last chance, Moineaux thought, *and I must make the most of it. Whether this be salvation or no, it is at least an opportunity, where there was none an hour ago. If that disgusting pig Lavinière hadn't thrown me out, I might have been sitting in some jumped-up bouillon Duval right now, watching him stuff his ugly face and mumble complaints about the quality of mass-produced carbon-paper, all at my expense! A new* Faust *might be a long shot, but I have no alternative, and I must say and do whatever I can to preserve the opportunity.*

"We are in agreement, then," Simon de Keramour said, placidly. His thin voice was reminiscent of elm-boughs stirring in a gentle wind, or the rustle of ancient pieces of paper shuffled on a desk-top.

"Our fates are bound together," Moineaux declared, staring at the empty glass from which he had already drained the dregs. He suddenly felt tired, as if a liter of blood had somehow been abstracted from his veins.

7

Moineaux took his copy of Simon de Keramour's play back to the Tragicomique in the *coupé*. He spent the journey-time reading Act Three, with a frown on his face, and did not notice what route they took in order to return to the city center, or even the direction from which they approached it.

The coachman got him to the Théâtre Tragicomique with plenty of time to spare before he had to make himself as the Gothic villain of *Le Chevalier Malcontent*, but the thanks he offered the man were a trifle understated. Content as he was with the economical journey-time, his mood was clouded by anxieties awakened by the third act of they play to whose production he had already committed himself.

Act Three of *Le Nouveau Faust* lacked nothing in melodrama; indeed, its climactic duel, fought between the two major characters while the young female lead looked on in dire apprehension, lent itself very well to the kind of staging in which Moineaux specialized. Until that point, there was little chance that the audience would be confused as to which character was which, even though the actors playing them had changed places, but the actor-manager was not entirely clear in his own mind which of the two the audience was supposed to favor in the duel–and the final scene that succeeded the duel only served, in his opinion, to increase that potential uncertainty.

In one sense, Simon de Keramour had done his very best to avoid the possibility of confusion. There was no second identity-exchange, and Mephistopheles–having won the duel in the body that had once been Jean Faust's–remained in that body while he made his concluding speech. On the other hand, the speech in question had far less to say about Jean Faust's fate, and the moral implications thereof, than it had about the lessons Mephistopheles had allegedly been forced to learn by his brief confinement in a frail human body.

Moineaux was not at all sure that this ending fit the play as well as either of two obvious alternatives that sprung readily enough to his mind. He could see that it might be thought to follow logically from the crucial dialogue in Act Two that had already caused him some anxiety, but he was not at all sure that the dialogue in question ought to remain as it was, or even remain in the play. In a *Faust*–even a revisionist *Faust*–Faust surely ought to be the central character, and Mephistopheles merely a means of granting his ambitious desires. Simon de Keramour seemed to have been seduced into a far greater interest in Mephistopheles than was necessary or politic.

On the other hand, Moineaux reminded himself, as he dropped the script on to the desk in his office, such a change of emphasis was not entirely injurious to his own part, in that he would begin his performance playing Faust but end it playing Mephistopheles.

He did not often go to the green room before a performance, but he found time to call in that evening. After a hundred cursory bows and lukewarm greetings, he managed to draw Lillette Fevret away from her devoted admirers for a few seconds.

"I wanted to let you know, my dear," he said, "that I have found a new play that is sure to redeem the company's flagging fortunes. It has a wonderful part for a young actress, playing two contrasted roles. I believe that you are ready now to take a leading role, and this one might have the potential to make you a star. I'm sure that you will be a great success."

54

"Really, Monsieur Moineaux?" the *ingénue* said, delightedly. "Do you really think it will make me a star?"

"I'm sure of it," Moineaux assured her. "The contract is not yet signed, but I shall be able tell the rest of the company tomorrow. You may give the good news to the Comte after the performance, of course, but please be discreet in talking to others. You may tell him that the play is called *Le Nouveau Faust*, and that it is by a brilliant young Breton who writes under the name of Simon de Keramour."

The inevitable result of his request that Lillette be discreet was that everyone in the green room had heard the news within five minutes. Paul Damas came to see Moineaux as he was putting on his make-up, to ask: "Is this new *Faust* the play that you promised me, *Maître*? Am I to play the new Faust himself?"

"You shall have two roles to play, Paul," Moineaux told him. "It will be the greatest challenge you have yet faced as an actor. In this version of the story, you see, Jean Faust–he is a Frenchman–trades bodies with Mephistopheles, imagining that the exchange will make him invulnerable to all Earthly harm. He is warned that the body has a single flaw, because it is the Devil's work, and therefore cannot be a perfect creation, but he is also assured that no mere mortal man will ever be able to detect the flaw. That turns out to be a trick, of course, for Mephistopheles retains the knowledge of exactly where the flaw is to be found, and is thus able to claim Faust's soul regardless. You will begin the play in the part of Mephistopheles, but end it as Faust, while I shall play the complementary roles. We shall have such fun with it, my boy! I feel more enthused about the prospect that I have about any play we have put on in the last three years."

"You always say that," Paul observed. "I don't doubt that you always mean it, of course. When do you hope to open it?"

"You shall read it for the first time tomorrow afternoon," Moineaux told him, "and study it closely all day Sunday, ready to read it through with the rest of the cast on Monday. The set-builders, scene-painters, seamstresses and poster-artists will be given their instructions tomorrow afternoon, and will set to work immediately. Rehearsals will begin on Wednesday next, and will take place every afternoon thereafter, except when there's a matinée performance of *Le Chevalier*. We shall open on the first Saturday in June."

"But that's only 15 days hence!" Paul protested. "How can you expect me to learn a part of that complexity and magnitude in a matter of days?"

"I have every confidence in you, Paul," Moineaux aid, calmly, "as I have in everyone else."

"We'll certainly have to rehearse it on a daily basis if we're to master the words," Paul remarked, in a manner that was slightly aggrieved, despite the compliment he had been paid. "That's not taking account of the ongoing adjustments you always delight in making. We'll have hardly any time to master the action-scenes, even if the set-builders work around the clock and the scene-shifters are willing to exchange the sets for the new play and *Le Chevalier* on a daily basis."

"*Le Chevalier Malcontent* will close on the Wednesday before *Le Nouveau Faust* opens," Moineaux said, firmly. "We'll have two days' full use of the complete set. There are only three scenes requiring complex action-sequences, of which only one–the final fight scene–is authentically demanding. You and I are old hands at sword-fighting by now, Paul; we're such veterans of false conflict that we could improvise the whole thing from scratch if we had to. If necessary, we'll adapt the moves contained in the fight that forms the climax of *Le Chevalier*. You'll have to remember, though, that–just for once–I'm supposed to win."

His attempt to lighten Paul's mood with the jocular tone of the last remark was unsuccessful, but it did not matter overmuch. They both had their final preparations to make for the performance of *Le Chevalier Malcontent*. After the final curtain, Moineaux shut himself away in his office, telling everyone that the contract for *Le Nouveau Faust* was not yet drawn up, and that he would not say another word about it until the document was properly signed and sealed.

Once the formalities had been tidied up, however—at eleven o'clock the following morning—and the cast was assembled to meet the author and receive their copies of the script, the muted protests began in earnest.

"How can the understudies possibly be expected to master the major parts alongside their own?" Hubert Marin complained. Marin, the oldest male actor in the company after Moineaux, had been the actor-director's regular understudy for years, and always complained bitterly that the work was as burdensome as it was futile. Moineaux had missed less than a dozen performances since 1880, although he had played a half a hundred with a high fever and almost as many with a fearful migraine.

"The understudies will doubtless do the best they can, Hubert," Moineaux replied, "but I don't expect miracles. If we have to open without fully-prepared understudies, we shall have to make certain that none of us falls ill. If anyone does, he or she will remember that the divine Sarah goes on every night with a wooden leg, and never utters a whimper of complaint."

"Even so," Marianne complained, "there's not time enough for the people planning two roles to master the complexities of their parts."

"I have absolute confidence in you, my dear, and the other leading players," Moineaux assured her.

Marianne was not put off so easily. "I don't worry for myself, of course," she said. "I've had more than 30 years of experience, and I can see at a glance that my own part is rather peripheral. Paul and Lillette are not used to parts of this complexity. How will they learn all the lines and moves specified here, let alone the changes you import during in the course of rehearsals?"

Before Moineaux could answer, Simon de Keramour interrupted. "Any changes we are compelled to make will be kept to an absolute minimum," he said. "Monsieur Moineaux and I are perfectly content with the play as it is."

This unexpected interpolation brought a sudden silence. The members of the company stared at the stranger in their midst, as startled by his temerity as they had been by his initial appearance.

The playwright did cut a rather strange figure. He was dressed in a conspicuously provincial suit, wearing eyeglasses whose lenses had been smoked to a deep brown color, and he had small wads of cotton wool stuffed into his ears.

"We shall content ourselves with those modifications that are absolutely necessary, to begin with," Moineaux confirmed. "With regard to necessary adjustments to the text, and to the careful integration of words and action, Monsieur de Keramour will be here every day, working closely with me to ensure that the piece is ready on time. We are fortunate to have this opportunity. I had to exert myself to the utmost yesterday to snatch Monsieur de Keramour's play from the very jaws of the Grand Guignol. I did not do that for my own benefit but for yours. I am on the verge of retirement, but all of you still have careers to build, or at least to preserve. You all know by now that *Le Chevalier Malcontent*, for all its merits as a play, has not contrived to catch the imagination of the fickle public. *Le Nouveau Faust* will not only succeed in doing that, but will succeed so spectacularly that it will be the making of everyone who has the honor to have a part in it, however small. In order to make that happen, though, we must all pull together. Hubert, if you are tired of serving as my understudy, perhaps the time has come to hand the responsibility to a younger man–Germain, perhaps."

"Oh no!" Marin was very quick to say. "I will do my very best, of course, *Maître!*"

There was a general echo of agreement.

Before that evening's performance of *Le Chevalier Malcontent*, the Comte de Farineux took the unusual step of leaving the green room in order to visit Moineaux in his office, having evidently cast a rapid eye over the script that Lillette Fevret had entrusted to him for safe-keeping.

"When Lillette told me last night, Monsieur Moineaux," he said, "that the great project you mentioned to me in the morning was yet another new *Faust*, I must confess that I was rather disappointed. I haven't had time to read the script thoroughly, but at first glance it certainly doesn't seem to me to be a great play. It's distinctly old-fashioned—and what's all this rubbish about evolution and progress in Act Two? Is that what you consider an apt scene for my darling Lillette? Playing a would-be scholar hardly constitutes a road to stardom."

"The would-be scholar is only one of her roles, sire," Moineaux pointed out. "You have doubtless observed that the other is a courtesan, explicitly described as a personification of lust. What an exercise in contrasts that will be! And what an opportunity for our dear *protégée* to broaden her range! Don't worry, Monsieur le Comte: she will be magnificent, and everyone will acknowledge the fact."

"So you're prepared to wager everything—and don't try to tell me that you'll have any resources left if this farce doesn't fly—on a new *Faust* by an unknown playwright? What I've read doesn't convince *me* that it's a work of genius."

"It needs a little work, that's true, sire," Moineaux conceded, "but almost all the work that needs to be done is concentrated in two scenes. One is the dialogue in Act Two between Marguerite and her teacher—who has been replaced, unknown to her, by Mephistopheles—to which you have already called attention. The other is the final scene, following Mephistopheles' victory in the climactic duel, in which the lessons of the drama are summarized."

"I haven't got that far," the Comte admitted.

"When you have, sire," Moineaux told him, "You'll immediately perceive that we might have to shift the focus back from Mephistopheles' reflections on his own plight to the fact and significance of Faust's damnation. We need something that will round off the plot with more *brio*, and a little more wit. Both repairs can be effected, I think, by modifying my own speeches. The essence of Lillette's part is not in her lines, which are perfectly adequate to her task, but her ability to play the two contrasting aspects of her double role with equal conviction. If she can do that–and I firmly believe that she can– she will establish her reputation as a serious actress at a single stroke. That is what I promised you; that is what I shall deliver. The play will be a success, Monsieur–both a *succès d'estime* and a commercial success."

The Comte nodded his head, but it did not seem to be an affirmative gesture. "And who, exactly, is this so-called Simon de Keramour?" he asked, dubiously. The playwright had returned to his home following the afternoon session rather than going to the green room.

"You will meet Monsieur de Keramour soon enough, sire," Moineaux said. "and I am sure that you will become the best of friends. He comes from an old Breton family–one that seems to have fallen on hard times, as so many Breton families have, but which retains the respect of its peers. I think he might be a worthy successor to my old friend Paul Féval. He has a house in one of the more venerable quarters of the city, and an excellent library. He also has an exceptionally fine pair of horses to draw his carriage–you will be interested to see them, I think."

8

The final item in the list of assurances that Moineaux had offered the Comte de Farineux proved to be correct. The Comte was, indeed, impressed by the quality of Simon de Keramour's carriage-horses–far more so than by the man himself, as it turned out.

The two men did not meet on the following day, which was Sunday, but they did meet at the first reading of the play on the Monday thereafter. It was not in consequence of the manifest eccentricity of the playwright's appearance that Moineaux's prediction that the Comte and he would become the best of friends was so quickly falsified. They greeted one another quite politely at first, when they settled down together to watch the first collective reading of the script, but by the time the actors had reached the mid-point of Act Two, however, it was obvious that a certain tension had developed between them. The Comte had begun to take exception to the intense interest that the author was taking in Lillette Fevret and the manner in which she delivered–or ought to deliver–her lines.

This situation went rapidly from bad to worse. The Comte's objection to the manner of the interaction between Simon de Keramour and Lillette-as-Marguerite was aggravated by a further order of magnitude when he was able to watch the playwright coaching her in her second role as lust personified. It was obvious to Moineaux–as it must have been to everyone else on stage–that there was rather more lust in the atmosphere than was contained in the character of the semi-reluctant courtesan.

Although it would be a ludicrous exaggeration to say that Simon de Keramour had fallen in love at first sight with Lillette Fevret–that being the kind of thing that only happens in melodramas–there was no doubt that the young playwright was strongly attracted to her. There was nothing unusual in that, given the way the *habitués* of the green room flocked around her and the manifest conviction with which Paul Damas played his love-scenes with her, but etiquette demanded that such attractions be expressed in within very narrow confines–and the Comte de Farineux believed even more passionately in that aspect of etiquette than any other. The gentlemen of the green room confined their effusions of admiration to the space within its defining walls, and Paul confined his to the stage. Outside of those protected environments, everyone was required to acknowledge that Lillette belonged, body and soul, to the Comte, and to behave accordingly.

Simon de Keramour evidently did not know these rules of conduct. In a situation that did not permit it, he addressed Mademoiselle Fevret in too informal a manner, praised her charms with excessive sincerity, and looked at her with naked desire. At times, he almost appeared to be paying court to her, as if she were free to receive suitors.

Moineaux chided himself for not having warned the author about the etiquette of rehearsals, but he could not imagine that it would have made any difference. The man was a writer, after all, and a Breton–and his pseudonym retained a magical "de" whose entitlements he seemed to be taking entirely seriously, despite the fact that no one else would.

It seemed extremely unlikely that the playwright's sentiments might be reciprocated in the least, but Lillette nevertheless seemed delighted with the fervor of the attention that Simon de Keramour was paying her. Moineaux no longer feared that the Comte would be able to carry her off to the Gambardi or the Bouffée any time soon, but he did become anxious that there might be trouble before the production opened between Monsieur de Keramour and the Comte.

In the interests of maintaining the harmony of his company, Moineaux felt that it was his duty to take Simon de Keramour to one side as soon as the run-through was complete, for an intensive discussion of the manner in which the text read when sounded aloud.

"Begin again," he said to the cast, as he led the playwright away. "Hubert, will you read my lines until I'm able to return."

Hubert Marin, who was playing Faust's servant, complained that he could not possibly talk to himself in the first act, so Moineaux asked Germain Querelle to do it instead. Querelle was playing the host of the cabaret in which the rejuvenated Faust pursued his new appetites, and had no dialogues with Moineaux's characters at all, but the actor-manager knew full well that if he had asked Germain first, Marin would have been offended, on the grounds that he was the senior member of the company and Moineaux's official understudy.

"What did you think of the reading, Monsieur de Keramour?" Moineaux asked his author, when he had drawn him into the wings.

"First rate, Monsieur Moineaux," the author replied. "Your company has brought my words to life, and I am profoundly grateful to you. Mademoiselle Fevret is perfect–exceptionally accomplished for one so young."

"Lillette is the youngest of three half-sisters who were the daughters of an actress and became actresses themselves," Moineaux observed. "Her mother died when she was very young, but Ernestine and Juliette, her sisters, took responsibility for her care and education. Lillette has spent her entire life in theaters, and knows the business from top to bottom. Ernestine and Juliette are both dead now, but Juliette survived long enough to see Lillette safely lodged at the Tragicomique. Juliette was famous in her day as a tragedienne, and must have regarded my humble company as a mere starting-point, but she was kind enough to give the appointment her whole-hearted blessing. Following her death, and one or two petty adventures, the Comte took over responsibility for Lillette's wellbeing, and he has looked after her very well."

"Like the father she never had?" the playwright queried, sarcastically.

"In a manner of speaking. She adores him. He can be an irritant presence, but he's a man of substance and style. Lillette needs him, and the Tragicomique needs him. I implore you to treat him with more than due deference and politeness."

"I shall do my utmost." Simon de Keramour's eyes were invisible behind his smoked lenses, but his mournful expression was still in place. It was not conducive to confidence in the forcefulness of his promises, even thought he was a Breton as well as a writer.

"I could find no fault with Lillette's performance myself," Moineaux said, steering the conversation back towards it proper subject, "but the burden of the play's *meaning* devolves almost entirely upon me, especially in my capacity as the humanized Mephistopheles. Paul's part might need a little work too, but it seems to me that my two key scenes will require more careful formulation. Lacking Paul's virile good looks and Lillette's charm and beauty, I have only my speeches with which to create an effect. Will you work on them with me, Monsieur?"

"I thought that they went very well," de Keramour retorted, frostily. "You're too modest, Monsieur Moineaux–you did the speeches full justice, and they sounded very well in your mouth. They will doubtless sound even better when you're in costume, playing to an audience. The impact of the final speech was much reduced, of course, because there was no preliminary duel; when it is placed in its rightful context it will surely move the audience to sober reflection on the play's central theme, as set out in Act Two."

"The duel itself makes for a stirring climax," Moineaux admitted, "and it will doubtless look very well when Paul and I have practiced the moves. When we're in costume, with deftly-placed blood-bags to be punctured at the crucial moments, it will be quite a spectacle–which is exactly why we might need a livelier summary thereafter. As for the setting out in Act Two, I wonder whether that might sit more comfortably within the narrative flow if it were slightly reshaped and refined. Lillette's contribution to the dialogue might be more effective if my own could be raised to a slightly higher pitch of clarity and excitement–without compromising the essential argumentative thrust of your discourse, naturally."

"On the contrary," the author replied, defiantly but always maintaining the insistent quietness of his voice. "To exaggerate your contribution would inevitably detract from Lillette's, and your part of the conversation is just as clear as hers. As for excitement, I have read that Monsieur Lamarck's lectures on evolution and progress at the Jardin des Plantes held his audience rapt for hours, purely by virtue of the thrilling quality of his ideas."

"I'm not sure that the reports in question are entirely to be trusted," Moineaux persisted, silkily, "and even if they could, we would have to bear in mind that he was addressing a very different audience in a very different era. If the success of the Grand Guignol tells us anything at all..."

"Is this the kind of collaboration that you offered me last Friday?" Simon de Keramour said, contriving to sound bitter despite the fact that he was talking in whispers, and seeming to stare accusingly despite the fact that his blue eyes were completely eclipsed by his brown spectacles. "Did you not sit in my study and lament the modern trend that led your rival directors to have scripts rewritten by hacks, in order to substitute mere sensation for the produce of intellect, or to issue reams of notes instructing their authors to play the vaudevillian? Did you not tell me that you had too much integrity and respect to wreak such brutality upon your authors' essential themes? Are you not fully aware that the reason I gave my play to you–the *only* reason that I gave my play to you–without even showing it to anyone else, is that you gave me your solemn word that you would not tamper with a single word or gesture without my express permission?"

This last assertion was an exaggeration, reflective of a slight misunderstanding, but Moineaux knew how carefully he had to tread. The contract he had given Simon de Keramour to sign contained a standard clause giving its director the right to modify the play as he saw fit, but it also included the clause he had been specifically asked to include, which specified that the author had the right to take the play back if any changes were made that had not been sanctioned by him. Moineaux needed Simon de Keramour's active participation and full cooperation if he was to get the play ready for its opening, let alone make a success of it in time to have any chance of saving the Tragicomique. He was all too well aware of the fact that if the Breton were to be stubborn in making difficulties, his company's last chance of survival might go up in smoke. Moineaux could not help wondering whether the author understood that very well, and had determined to take full advantage of the unusual situation.

"In view of the limited time at our disposal," Moineaux conceded, soothingly, "it's probably best to leave the script as it is for the time being. We'll say no more about it, until we have a better idea how the piece works when the words are

65

supplemented by the action. May I ask you one favor, though?"

"What is it?" de Keramour countered, warily.

"I wish you would do your utmost to help Paul master his part. I need to concentrate on my own, while Lillette has the Comte to read with her while she practices in private, but Paul has a part more complex than any that he has played before. He will need someone to read with him as frequently as possible, at least for the next four or five days. As the author of the piece, you have a unique insight into the transitions of his performance and the significance of his speeches. He needs your help, Monsieur de Keramour, and I hope that you will be enthusiastic to provide it. It might make a considerable difference to the early performances of the play–especially the one on which the first reviews will be based."

The author hesitated for a moment–a moment, perhaps, when his new-found jealousy of the Comte de Farineux increased by a further degree, as he imagined the old soldier and Lillette practicing his lines together. Then he said: "Yes, I shall be glad to do that. I understand the necessity. Will Madame Jonquille be able to cope, do you think?"

"Easily," Moineaux assured him. "Her experience is not as vast as my own, but it's certainly abundant. Hubert will be pleased to assist her if the need arises, and Germain too. Their parts are relatively undemanding, by their own high standards. Now, I must get back to the reading, or else poor Germain will be quite out of breath. It might be better if you stayed in the wings rather than rejoining the Comte in the stalls–it will be less distracting for both of you."

"Perhaps it will," the author conceded, only a little reluctantly. "Does the Comte make a habit of coming to readings and rehearsals, by the way? I would have thought that there were many other pressures on his valuable time."

"Oh no," Moineaux told him. "Today is quite an exception–but I had told him about your play in advance, you see, and Lillette gave him her copy of the script to read. He was anxious to meet you. I doubt that you'll see him again before the final dress rehearsal, perhaps even the first performance."

Simon de Keramour seemed satisfied with this assurance. It transpired, however, that the Comte de Farineux was less than satisfied with the same circumstance. The hero of the Second Empire felt a sense of urgency sufficient to bring him to the actor-manager's dressing-room yet again that evening, while Moineaux was being made up as the villain of *Le Chevalier Malcontent.*

"I don't deny that young de Keramour's something of a playwright," the Comte said, "but it turns out that he's also something of a perverse popinjay and a budding Don Juan. I can't blame him for being thunderstruck by Lillette, but I need to be sure that he understands the rules of the game. Were he to overstep the mark, I might have to polish my sword one more time, even though that sort of thing isn't supposed to be done any more."

"You have no cause whatsoever for anxiety, Monsieur le Comte," Moineaux assured the veteran of Sedan. "The boy is deeply impressed, of course, but he's a gentleman through and through. Chivalry never entirely died out in Brittany, you know, and he would no more dream of exceeding the bounds of propriety than of selling his soul to the Devil. In any case, I'm here—and shall be ever-present from now on—to play the role of a fond paternal guardian. I assure you, Monsieur le Comte, that Lillette will be perfectly safe from all impropriety while there is breath in my body. Always remember that she loves you very dearly!"

"You have a point there," the Comte conceded. "This de Keramour fellow is poor, you say, despite the fine horses pulling his coach?"

"I'm not in a position to make an accurate judgement," Moineaux said, "but my impression is that he's clinging to the last remnants of a once-rich inheritance that has faded away for lack of renewal. His house in Paris is no workman's hovel, but it's something of a ruin and he keeps it very dimly lit."

"Where is it, exactly?" the Comte asked, perhaps desirous of knowing exactly where to send his card if the occasion did arise.

"I'm afraid that I can't tell you the address," Moineaux said, honestly. "I've been there and back again, but only once; I was so busy during the transit that I paid little or no attention to the route."

"Who are his friends?" the Comte persisted.

"He doesn't appear to know anyone in Paris, save for a few dusty antiquarians. Did you notice how pale he is? That's the legacy of long and lonely scholarship."

"I did," the Comte confirmed. "The fellow's in the early stages of consumption, if I'm any judge. And those hidden eyes! A laudanum-drinker, I suspect, or an injector of morphine. He'd shatter, I think, if he were exposed to a loud enough noise without the protective benefit of his earplugs, and he'd surely blow away in a brisk wind."

The Comte appeared to be trying to reassure himself that he had absolutely nothing to fear from the playwright's rivalry, in the matter of Lillette's affections. That was not an opinion Moineaux wanted to undermine in any degree whatsoever, and he was certainly not disposed to remind the older man that young women often found a certain unhealthiness romantically attractive in a man, especially if the man were a poet or a playwright.

"You mustn't read too much into the boy's excitement, sire," Moineaux murmured, almost as if he were speaking to the playwright, with due consideration for his tender ears. "This will be the first time he's had a play produced, and he has even more riding on the prospect of its success than anyone else, including me. And now you must excuse me, Comte; I'm due on stage in little more than a minute."

On that different and more generous stage, he added, silently, to himself, *where a man's fellow players respond to his cues in a much more reliable fashion, and where the dénouement always works out in the interests of poetic justice.*

Act Two
Monsieur Moineaux's Mishap

9

When the curtain came down on that night's perform-ance of *Le Chevalier Malcontent*, Stéphane Moineaux found himself in the unaccustomed position of being able to revel in solitude for a while. No one came to see him in his office, and when he left the theater, the caretaker refrained from mutter-ing any complaint, however muted, about the bloodstains on the stage or any other inconvenience. For once, Moineaux was able to go to bed early–but he took Monsieur de Keramour's script with him, so that he could study it carefully while his candle lasted.

He had read the play through a dozen times by now, and heard it read aloud twice. On the first few readings, he had concentrated its potential appeal to the public, and the prob-lems of staging it, but wanted to delve beneath the surface, into its deeper meanings and more profound potential. The afternoon's readings by the players in his company had given him a better sense of what might yet be done with the play once he was in a firmer position to dictate the terms of a thor-ough revision. What he wanted to do now was immerse him-self more fully in its philosophy.

The legend of Faust had undergone a great many literary metamorphoses since its first publication in Germany in the late 16th century and its first dramatization in England by Christopher Marlowe. The original moral of the tale had been the contention that the desire for worldly knowledge would lead inexorably to damnation. The assumption underlying that contention was that any man who focused his intelligence on material matters rather than spiritual ones was committing a deadly sin, yielding to one of the Devil's subtlest temptations–

but that moral had been formed before the revelations wrought by Galileo, Kepler and Newton, let alone those achieved in the present century by the followers of Lavoisier in the field of chemistry, the followers of Lamarck and Buffon in the field of biology, and the followers of Pasteur in the field of medicine.

In 1899, Moineaux thought, the quest for secular knowledge could no longer seem in the least futile or inglorious, even to the kind of audience that reveled in the Grand Guignol's horrors and theatrical effects. Many of the traditional horrors of the Gothic imagination had now become so clichéd and so ridiculous that they could only be staged as black comedy–to the extent that it made perfect sense, in *fin-de-siècle* Paris to have a Théâtre Tragicomique.

The inevitable historical consequence of the revelatory fruits of the Faustian quest had been a gradual but very distinct movement in the definition of Faust's character in successive versions of the legend, from foolish victim to problematic hero. His bargain with the Devil–whose essence was unaffected by quibbles as to whether Mephistopheles ought to be reckoned as a pseudonym of Lucifer himself, or as a subsidiary minion–had ceased to function as a symbol of tacit alienation from God, and had begun to symbolize a bold stroke of reckless daring. Instead of Faust's ultimate damnation being as just as it was inevitable, there were numerous modern versions of the story that reckoned it horribly unjust. When that damnation was achieved nowadays, it was usually represented as stark tragedy rather than stern justice; in many other versions, Faust was triumphantly redeemed from threatened destruction.

Simon de Keramour's version offered a further recomplication of this evolving pattern, and was thus fully entitled to represent itself as a *new* Faust. It was traditional, in the sense that Faust died at the end, presumably damned to Hell, and also traditional in the sense that he seemed to deserve his damnation, but the reasons why Simon de Keramour's Faust deserved damnation were quite different from the reasons that the author of the 16th century *Faustbuch* had had in mind. Here, Faust's quest for worldly knowledge–for *scientific* knowledge–was seen as entirely virtuous, and profitable to his fellow men. His willingness to trade his soul for further knowledge of that kind was represented as a noble gesture of heroic self-sacrifice. When the bargain was made, however, Simon de Keramour's Faust was tricked. The exact nature of the trick was complicated, though, and one of the functions with which de Keramour's dialogue struggled to cope was that of spelling it out in such a way that the audience could understand it and appreciate it fully.

The most superficial aspect of Faust's entrapment was that he was promised effective invulnerability to harm as well as the renewal of his youth, both of those being innate properties of Mephistopheles' demonic body–but Mephistopheles knew perfectly well where its fatal flaw was, and knew exactly how to deliver the only kind of fatal blow that Faust's borrowed form could possibly sustain. It was by this means that the demon, temporarily confined to Faust's frail form, was able to put a premature end to Faust's adventure in the climactic duel.

At a deeper level, however, the scholar's betrayal was far more tortuous than that convenient plot-twist. The real point of the exchange of bodies was that, in making it, Faust lost exactly what he had sought to gain. He had been tempted into thinking of the exchange as a matter of *means*: that a return to youth and vigor would give him the time and fortitude to continue his scientific studies and wring many more achievements therefrom. The exchange of bodies did, indeed, give him those means–but it also took away his will to use them.

When he acquired a demonic body, Faust acquired the demonic appetites and desires incarnate in that exotic flesh. He no longer had the slightest motivation to scientific research or philosophical cogitation. The only interest that remained to him was pleasure, and he immediately began to devote the gift for which he had bargained entirely to the cultivation of sensuality. Simon de Keramour's Faust was by no means displeased by the rewards of his bargain–which, with the aid of the courtesan who functioned as a personification of lust, were by no means inconsiderable, but that was because he had forgotten the purpose for which he had made it. In forgetting his heroic purpose, he was supposed to have forfeited his right to the audience's moral sympathy, thus warranting damnation.

Moineaux was by no means certain that a typical Tragicomique audience would *actually* lose sympathy for Faust in the fashion that the script's author supposed, even if they grasped the author's intention. Indeed, he knew full well that the majority of the members of such an audience would greatly prefer the rejuvenated Faust to the old scholar, and would take great delight in his languorous dalliance with the mildly reluctant courtesan. The greater number of that majority would know as they did so, however, that they were supposed to feel guilty about it, and it would not affect their awareness of the wry propriety of the ending or their understanding of the symbolism of the "fatal flaw" in his invisible armor. The real problem with the complexity of the argument was not the danger that it might be misunderstood, Moineaux decided, but the fact that it was not the real essence of the play.

The most awkward consequence of the trick played by Mephistopheles on Jean Faust, in terms of essential artistry as well as practical stagecraft, was that Simon de Keramour's own interest had shifted from exploration of what the mutual exchange of forms did to Faust to what it meant to Mephistopheles. While Faust received temporary custody of a body whose demonic quality subverted the intellect and nobility that had formerly made him a scientist, Mephistopheles was consigned to a body that was no longer equipped with the violent appetites that had made him a demon. He, too, lost the will that had formerly driven him to his own peculiar achievements, and found himself condemned, not to Hell, but to philosophy.

While Faust became infatuated with the courtesan, Mephistopheles became fascinated with her counterpart, the scholar. Introduced by his habitation of Faust's body and brain to an informed appreciation of the actuality of Creation, in all its wondrous intricacy, Mephistopheles found his new appetites as overwhelming in their fashion as Faust found his. That new consciousness, and everything that came with it, was the motive force of the wistful speeches that Mephistopheles made in Act Two, in response to prompts from Marguerite, the eager pupil of the man whose form he had adopted. It was also the theme of his climactic speech, following Faust's extinction and presumed damnation.

The dialogue in Act Two did not constitute a love scene in any conventional sense–certainly not in the same sense that the scene in Act Two involving Faust with the courtesan for the first time was a "love scene"–but it was a scene in which Marguerite contrived to awaken in Mephistopheles sensations that he had ever experienced before, which allegedly offered him a kind of ecstasy of whose existence he had never dreamed, and gave him the opportunity to offer Marguerite educative advice that Jean Faust could never have given her.

The scene in Act Two certainly needed rewriting, in Moineaux's opinion. The supposed outburst of ecstasy seemed superfluous as well as difficult to express, and the whole exchange needed to be wittier and less intellectually pretentious. Even so, the actor could not help being intrigued by the basic argument of the dialogue. Marguerite, having struggled through the Chevalier de Lamarck's *Recherches sur l'organisation des corps vivants*–which had contained the first sketch of the ideas subsequently elaborated in *Philosophie zoologique*–questioned Faust on the implications of the idea that all organisms were possessed of an innate impulse to improvement, which was allegedly the motor of the evolution that had produced the rich complexity of life on Earth from the primitive beginnings of microscopic single-celled organisms. Was there only one path of improvement, she asked, whose culmination was man? If not–as, for instance, seemed to be implied by the example of birds, blessed with the gift of flight at the expense of manipulative skill–then how was one to decide which the best path might be? And how was one to decide how human beings themselves–especially the female of

73

the species–ought to direct their impulse to improvement? Had the Revolution of 1789 been an expression of that impulse or an aberration? Was Napoleon a better expression, or an interruption?

Simon de Keramour's Mephistopheles tried to answer all these questions very earnestly, but the audience had to guess what Jean Faust might have said instead. Stéphane Moineaux wanted *his* Mephistopheles to give a little more attention to more intimately personal matters, and to address them in a lighter spirit. Indeed, he was determined that *his* Mephistopheles actually would do that–if not on the first night then as a result of a gradual process of evolution that would be fully expressive of an innate impulse to improvement.

Simon de Keramour's Mephistopheles also brought his own agenda to the discussion in Act Two by explaining–not as briefly as a Tragicomique audience might desire–some of the things he had seen while his commission as a messenger of Hell had allowed him freedom to roam the exotic expanses of the universe revealed by modern science. This speech was undoubtedly derivative of the cosmic voyage sequence in Gustave Flaubert's *Tentation de Saint Antoine*, but it was decisively different in being more insulting to the pretensions of the New Testament's Devil than the vainglory of the Old Testament's God. Moineaux had already begun making mental notes for its revision, on the grounds that more satire needed to be injected into it if it were not simply to be discarded. Either move, he firmly believed, would still be respectful of Simon de Keramour's ambitions, and would assist them to a better fulfillment.

Moineaux understood that the central tragedy of the play's climax, in the author's eyes, was not Faust's death, which was merely a final obliteration of hopes and ambitions that had already been betrayed and spoiled, but the end of Mephistopheles' mission. The real tragedy of the climax, as it was presently constructed, was Mephistopheles' necessary loss of Faust's human privileges–frail and fugitive as the shell might be in which they were housed–in destroying the monster that he had created by trickery. Mephistopheles delivered his final speech in the knowledge that now Jean Faust was dead and damned, he would have to become a virile demon again himself: a creature entirely driven by the appetites of his baser self, unable to sustain the higher motives and searching intelligence he had briefly acquired, but equally unable to erase the memory of having once known them. By this means, Mephistopheles was condemned–and *knew* himself to be condemned, at least while he made that final speech, as his humanity faded away–to a worse Hell than he had been in before.

Even if this aspect of the tragedy were to be given its due, however, Moineaux's opinion was that a much more even balance needed to be struck with the demolition of Jean Faust's dreams and ambitions. The achievement of that better balance, however, posed a considerable practical problem, given that one of the two characters had to perish in the duel, leaving only one to formulate the final lament.

As he turned over the last page of the well-thumbed script yet again, and glanced sideways to measure the brief interval that had still to elapse before his candle guttered out, Moineaux wondered again whether the play might reach a more dramatic conclusion, and would also make better sense, if the re-exchange of identities were accomplished as soon as the fatal sword-stroke were delivered.

It would, Moineaux knew, be asking a lot of a typical Tragicomique audience to understand what was happening if a dead man were to get up again while the man who had just killed him fell down dead–but wasn't the logical outcome of the duel that as soon as Paul-as-Faust fell, Moineaux-as-Mephistopheles should clutch at his own heart, and fall in exactly the same fashion? Shouldn't Paul then to rise to his feet, no longer Paul-as-Faust but Paul-as-Mephistopheles-again, and deliver the final tragic oration, even as his consciousness of having been human, and his consciousness of the cost of his loss of that humanity, slowly ebbed away. Except, of course, that perhaps it should not be an isolated oration, but rather something more dazzlingly complex, involving an active interaction with Lillette's character–who ought, perhaps, to undergo a transformation of her own in response...

Moineaux set the script down on his night-stand and put his head back on the pillow. He did not bother to snuff out his candle, knowing that it was on the brink of extinction. He knew that his consideration of the problem of the final scene was still confused by the egotistic desire to retain the final speech for his own character, and also by the fact that he had had a long day, and had become very tired by the time he reached the play's coda. He knew, as he contemplated the magnitude and multifaceted nature of the difficulty, that he would do better to leave serious grappling with it to another time. He did resolve, though, that if due consideration *were* to persuade him that it would make more sense artistically for Paul's character to deliver the final judgement than for his own to do it, then that must be the eventual outcome–whether Simon de Keramour approved or not.

There would come a time, later if not sooner, when it would no longer be practical for Simon de Keramour to withdraw his script and take it to another director. Once the play had opened, the only people who could determine the words that were actually spoken on stage, not only in the final scene but all the scenes leading up to it, were the person who spoke the lines and the director to whom that person was responsible. When the actor and director were the same person, it made the business of amendment even simpler, though not necessarily easier.

As he formed that thought, Moineaux's candle went out, but he did not fall asleep immediately. There was too much on his mind, and he had to let go of it by slow degrees, knowing that it would come back to him in his dreams–but he was used to that. It was an inevitable aspect of the burden of his responsibility as the master of the Tragicomique.

10

The readings and rehearsals made as much progress as Moineaux could reasonably expect in the course of the following ten days. The impulse to improvement was forceful, but the play's evolution was a problematic process beset by many hitches. As Marguerite and her covertly-transformed tutor observed in the course of their dialogue in Act Two, the consequences of there being more than one possible road of improvement extended beyond the agonies of choice to the inevitability of conflict, and all roads to improvement were liberally strewn with obstacles and obstructions.

Moineaux's attempts to persuade Simon de Keramour to license even slight changes in his script were met with stern resistance, and he got little support from his cast, who were having difficulty enough learning the lines as they were, without accommodating serial alterations. In other respects, however, the author proved a great asset. As requested, he worked intensively with Paul Damas, not merely schooling him in his part but–more importantly–helping him to master the sequences of action in his fight scenes.

Paul's involvement in two duels provided key melodramatic high-points, and the inflated expectations of modern audiences meant that such fight scenes now required exceedingly complex arrangement. Moineaux had never hired a specialist fight-arranger, automatically assuming the responsibility for such work in his capacity as director, but he had so many other things to occupy his time if the play were to be made ready in a fortnight that it was a great relief to him when Simon de Keramour proved very enthusiastic to involve himself fully in the staging of his play. The author was able to school Paul and his first opponent–a bravo played by Fernand Cornu–in concert, but necessity required him to stand in for Moineaux during much of the preparation of the second and climactic duel.

The playwright proved to be a very clever swordsman, at least in terms of stage-fighting, easily able to take either part in a choreographed duel in order to demonstrate to the actors exactly what needed to be done and to put them through their paces. His earplugs seemed very efficient in protecting him from the sound effects accompanying the duels.

"Where did you learn to feign fencing so skillfully?" Moineaux asked the author, after watching the final phase of a session that left the Breton and Paul equally breathless. "Pretending to fight requires greater cleverness and delicacy than actually fighting, so I can't believe that you're simply transferring skills that you learned from an ordinary fencing-master."

"I've had some training of that sort," Simon de Keramour admitted, vaguely, "but I was never interested in the sport, let alone in military service. I seem to have a natural facility for pretense–and I must confess that I'm enjoying the work. I've produced my play so many times in the theater of my mind that I must have practiced my duels a hundred times in my sleep."

"I'm exceedingly grateful to have found such a multi-talented author," Moineaux told him, following his customary routine of diplomatic flattery. "Not only will Paul be ready for the opening night, but he'll be a more skillful performer in perpetuity by virtue of your input. Young Fernand will also benefit tremendously."

Instead of accepting the compliment gratefully, however, Simon de Keramour looked sharply at his employer from behind his smoked lenses and said: "I have no worries about Paul or Fernand–but I think that you might benefit from more practice. The second duel is the more demanding of the two, and by far the more important to the play. It would be a pity if Paul's improvement were not matched by his opponent."

"I've been fighting duels on stage since the heyday of the Second Empire," Moineaux told him, trying hard to retain a mild tone. "I have an exceptional memory for steps, and need not practice as hard as the younger members of the troupe. For the last two years and more I've clashed swords with Paul every night of the week, with occasional matinées thrown in, and I can assure you that if he is master of his moves, I shall match him stroke for stroke."

"Even so," de Keramour persisted, "I wish that you would let me take you through the fight on a daily basis, and then let me watch you repeat the moves with Paul."

"If I can find the time," Moineaux promised, doing his level best to feign sincerity–although he was not lying in the strictest sense, given that he knew how difficult it would be to find the time even if he made every effort, "I shall certainly make it a priority."

Moineaux divined that the author's eagerness in this particular respect was not entirely born of anxiety about his lack of preparation. He recognized that Simon de Keramour's intensive involvement in the more physically-demanding aspects of the production–for he was just as ready to lend a hand when the scene-shifters were struggling to work their multiple transformations–helped to discharge the tension that built up in him whenever he was close to Lillette Fevret.

What Moineaux had said to the Comte turned out to be true; Simon de Keramour *was* a perfect gentleman, not in the modern Parisian sense but in a fashion that had become obsolete centuries before, except perhaps in the romantic and faux-nostalgic fancies of Breton writers like Paul Féval. The author treated Lillette with the utmost courtesy–to an extent that became a running joke within the company–but that repression of his increasingly-heated passion only helped to intensify the emotional inferno.

Moineaux, on the other hand, had his own deep-seated reasons for remaining relentlessly busy. As the days sped by, so avidly consumed by the hectic roundabout of rehearsing one play and performing another, the actor-director was able to forget, often for hours at a time, that in terms of his career and finances he was a man on the brink of drowning, who had but one straw left to clutch, and that a frail one. For the greater part of every day he was able to avoid giving a single moment's thought to the possibility that his new Faust might

79

simply fail, opening to a house that was less than full and losing numbers every night thereafter. That prospect was, for him, literally beyond the scope of contemplation. While he was a feverishly busy actor-manager with one play to manage and another to prepare Stéphane Moineaux had a *raison d'être*; he flatly refused to entertain the horrid thought that if he were to lose that role, he would effectively cease to exist, becoming a kind of void that was abhorred by nature and artifice alike.

It was not, therefore, with anxious dread, but with simple pride that Moineaux watched his various *protégés* and *protégées* ease themselves into their new parts and bring them to life. Paul, as he had anticipated, relished the unprecedented range of his part, and worked conscientiously on seeming to be an entirely different person once he had forsaken the role of Mephistopheles in order to take that of the rejuvenated Faust. Moineaux had not anticipated that Marianne would be nearly so obliging, given the implicitly-demeaning character of both her roles, but she worked as hard on the double part as her daily consumption of strong liquor permitted.

At first, Lillette seemed far happier as the courtesan who answered Faust's new desires than the intellectually-curious pupil, and gave the impression that she would be happier still when she were able to play the more extravagant role in a much slighter costume than the clothes she wore to rehearsals. In time, though–thanks to her own efforts rather than the encouragement that the Comte attempted to provide–she became equally comfortable in the role of the female scholar. One of the pupil's key scenes was played opposite Marianne, and two others opposite Moineaux–first in his role as Faust and later in his role as Mephistopheles–and she eventually began to give the impression that she could and would make the most of all three.

As with his fight scene with Paul, Moineaux was not able to rehearse his two scenes with Lillette as often as he would have liked, and he was pleased when she did not beg him to spend more time on them. Indeed, as the second week of rehearsals drew toward its close, Lillette even ventured the suggestion to him that it ought be possible to expand her part by developing her contribution to the scene in Act Three in which she confronted the new Faust. Although Moineaux thought that there were other scenes whose need for further development was much greater, he encouraged her to talk to Simon de Keramour about the possibility, thinking that she might succeed in persuading him to accept the principle that his script ought to be open to modification–and that once the principle was established, Moineaux's genius as a rewriter would come into its own.

The work on the new play went so well, in the end, that by the time the curtain came down on *Le Chevalier Malcontent*–three days before *Le Nouveau Faust* was due to open–the mood of the entire company displayed a highly unusual uniformity, replete with confidence and anticipation. When the Comte de Farineux invited the author and the two leading members of the company to a dinner party at the Hôtel de Farineux on the Thursday, Moineaux only hesitated for a moment before accepting, on behalf of Marianne and Simon as well as himself. He knew that the Comte's reasons for inviting the author included the hope of finding out something about his background that would work to his advantage, and the determination to use the glamour of his social prestige and the fact of his present authority over Lillette to make the author feel small, but he did not think it would do Simon de Keramour any harm to be subjected to such pressure.

There was a full dress rehearsal on the Thursday afternoon, on a set that was virtually identical to the one that would be installed on the first night. It served to expose two dozen minor problems, but no major ones. Lillette and the three invitees to the Comte's *soirée* went home to dress for the occasion in an optimistic mood. They reconvened within the hour, but the three invited guests arrived separately at the Hôtel de Farineux and did not immediately flock together. They had been so close to one another during the previous ten days that time apart and conversation with people uninvolved in the

Tragicomique's adventure seemed a luxury to be savored. Moineaux did make a half-hearted attempt to establish himself by Simon de Keramour's side in the role of guide and advisor, but it was strategically frustrated when he was engaged in conversation by the Comte's sister, the widowed Madame de Vernier, and her dear friend Monsieur Léchelier.

"I hear that you've been reduced to putting on yet another version of *Faust*, Monsieur Moineaux," Madame de Vernier said, displaying the lack of tact for which she was justly notorious. "Don't you think that we've had far too many of them already?"

"A superfluity of *Fausts* is undoubtedly a theoretical possibility," Moineaux conceded, politely, "but I think there might be room for one more, provided that it is sufficiently original."

"Will you be playing Faust or Mephistopheles?" Monsieur Léchelier asked.

"Monsieur Moineaux is playing both of them," Madame de Vernier cut in, before the actor-manager could open his mouth. "Young Paul Damas is doing likewise, playing Mephistopheles when Monsieur Moineaux is Faust, and *vice versa*. Our dear Lillette is also playing a duel role, as a *grisette* and a courtesan—but she is very well used to that, is she not?"

This was monumentally unfair to Lillette, who had never been a working girl and was not now, properly speaking, a courtesan. "Monsieur de Keramour's Marguerite is not a *grisette*, Madame de Vernier," Moineaux said, wearily. "She is the daughter of a thoroughly respectable family, who desires an education in order that she might escape the straitjacket of convention—the play is set in 1804, you see, Monsieur Léchelier, with the Empire new-born and the 1789 Revolution still fresh in memory. All things must have seemed possible then, I suppose. You must have spent your own youth in an analogous situation, Madame de Vernier, while the Second Empire was still a fledgling and memories of 1848 were still a trifle raw—but the educational opportunities open to women must have seemed far less exciting the second time around, and I cannot blame you for thinking them far beneath your dignity."

While Madame de Vernier bridled, despite the fact that she was having trouble figuring out the exact dimensions of the insult she had been offered, Léchelier said: "This new playwright of yours is something of a character, I see–although I suppose it's a mercy that he isn't clad in bicycle shorts." Alfred Jarry had also been invited to one of the Comte's *soirées* when Moineaux had put on one of his plays–disastrously–the previous year, and had made an impact of sorts.

"Monsieur de Keramour comes from a very old Breton family," Moineaux explained. "Very ancient aristocratic lineages have a tendency to produce sensitive offspring nowadays, do they not? Madame de Vernier must be very relieved to come from more robust stock."

"To come to a dinner-party in smoked lenses, wearing earplugs, is more akin to rudeness than eccentricity," the Comte's sister opined. "In any case, Monsieur le Comte has researched the matter, and he says that there is no such title as de Keramour, and that the name appears to have been borrowed from some trashy novel. One can readily understand why a person might write a scandalous play under a pseudonym, but to employ one in society is tasteless and impolite. Do you know what the man's real name is, Monsieur Moineaux?"

"As it happens, I don't," Moineaux said, quietly appalled by the brutality of the lady's attempted espionage. "Nor have I seen the color of his blood, although I firmly believe it to be as blue as his eyes. I sometimes wonder, though, whether his protestations of relative poverty might be more akin to those of a Rockefeller comparing himself to Croesus than those of a man who lacks the means to keep his cellar and his library fully-stocked. He handles a sword very well, you know. I don't think I could have found a better fencing-coach in Paris for young Paul–although I dare say that your brother would have been more than adequate, were he not so insistent that his weapon has been sheathed for good."

Again Madame de Vernier looked daggers at him, although she still could not quite determine why Moineaux's observations were anything but harmlessly innocent. Moineaux took advantage of the lapse in the conversation to excuse himself, and he swiftly made his way to the fireplace, where Simon de Keramour was standing slightly apart from a group of hardy theater-goers, as if he had attempted but not quite succeeded to ease himself into it. "I'm sorry, Simon," he said, in a whisper even quieter than the one he normally used in addressing the author. "The Comte does not seem to have given you a very enthusiastic advertisement to his sister or his friends. If you find yourself seated next to Madame de Vernier at dinner–as you very well might–don't let her upset you. Don't bother to try to win her over, and don't feel the slightest obligation to answer any of her impertinent questions. Let it all wash over you, and try to enjoy the food."

The playwright nodded his head, but in a rather negligent fashion. His shielded eyes were firmly fixed–albeit at a respectful distance–on Lillette Fevret.

"Be careful, my friend," Moineaux murmured. "Inexperienced as she is, she's been playing a role since the day she learned to walk and talk, and she's mastered it thoroughly. She's a romantic on stage, because that's what playwrights always make of *ingénues*, but in life she's a realist through and through."

This time, Simon de Keramour turned to stare at him, almost as resentfully as Madame de Vernier, although the Breton was perfectly competent to decipher the half-hidden meanings lurking beneath the surface of Moineaux's speech. Instead of taking offence, he said; "You're wrong, Monsieur Moineaux. You're not quite the judge of people you believe yourself to be. It's the realist that's the role, and the romantic that's the truth. Lillette's days as the Comte's *protégée* are numbered. He's known that for some time, I think."

"I stand corrected, my friend," Moineaux said, with a slight sigh. "Sometimes, an actor-manager is too close to the members of his company to see them clearly. Writers sometimes have the same trouble with their characters."

The smoked lenses hid de Keramour's eyes almost completely, but his pale cheeks showed no vestige of color and his brow did not furrow in the slightest. "We *are* friends, Monsieur Moineaux," he said. "Better friends than you know, I think. You're anxious for the fortunes of my play because you're anxious for the fortunes of your theater, but there's no need. It will be a success–a sensation, even. The combination of my words and your art will make the new Mephistopheles a triumph. I wasn't entirely sure of that until today, but I am now. I'm very grateful to you, Monsieur Moineaux, for giving me this opportunity. I think we shall both profit from it, provided that you heed your own advice."

Moineaux was slightly taken aback by the final comment. "Which advice?" he queried.

"Be careful," Simon de Keramour said, flatly–and then he slipped away, leaving the actor-manager to narrow his eyes the way Madame de Vernier sometimes did when she was forced to wonder exactly how and why she had been rebuked. After that, Moineaux was perversely glad to see that the Comte de Farineux *had* taken the trouble to seat the playwright between his appalling sister and one of his most trusted friends, while he had set Moineaux two places to his own left, with the lovely Lillette in between them.

"Your performance this evening has been perfect, my dear," Moineaux whispered to her, as dessert was served, "despite the necessity of improvising your lines and gestures. I hope you'll forgive me if I congratulate myself, on the grounds that you have been my attentive pupil–and I hope you'll forgive me for hoping that you'll continue to play your role for as long as it pleases its audience."

"It's no use pretending, my dear Monsieur Faust," she whispered in reply, "that you're a demon in disguise–even one who has had to take on the burden of human intelligence. You're more convincing in that role than Paul is as a human with demon passions, but I know who and what you really

85

are." She smiled so broadly as she finished this speech that there was not the slightest possibility of Moineaux taking offense. He smiled in his turn–conspiratorially, because he was certain that the Comte de Farineux had not overheard a single word of the exchange. When he looked at the opposite side of the table, however, he saw Simon de Keramour staring at the two of them, and was certain that–despite the earplugs the writer was wearing–the playwright *had* heard and understood every word.

11

When the day of the opening night brightened into fervent golden sunlight unobscured by clouds, Stéphane Moineaux was mildly surprised to find himself in a devil-may-care mood as he leapt out of bed. He could not remember ever having looked forward to a production at the Tragicomique as much as he was looking forward to the new *Faust*. All the birds of ill-omen that had been circling overhead for months, if not years, suddenly seemed to have faded into the background of his life, becoming mere specks in a dazzling sky.

Advance ticket sales had been reasonably good, and Moineaux expected that a much longer queue than usual would form as 7:30 in the evening drew near. The Grand Guignol was in the fourth week of Monsieur Bonis-Characle's *Les Loups*, which had gleaned relatively mediocre reviews and had been in no danger of having its run cut short by the censor; it was still playing to three-quarters full houses, but the ruthless Méténier would undoubtedly axe it as soon as the next play on his long list was ready.

The morning post brought several letters from various creditors, agitating for payment more urgently than usual, but Moineaux threw them casually aside and sat down to breakfast with a light heart. He went to the theater early, in order to supervise the completion and dressing of the set, but no serious problems arose. As his fellow-players arrived, one by one, he greeted them all warmly, and was glad to find them equally confident and cheerful. Paul and Lillette were agog with excitement, and Marianne had shed the hitherto-perennial vagueness that was the chief legacy of her excessive fondness for liquor.

"This will be the saving of us, won't it, Stéphane?" the former leading lady murmured, as he kissed her hand. "A new *Faust*, a new dawn. If I'm to be reduced to playing mothers from now until I die, then I'm reconciled to my fate. We shall be safe, you and I–and safety is as precious a thing as beauty, in its way."

Moineaux had not had an opportunity to talk to Marianne at the Comte's dinner-party. In fact, to be strictly accurate, he had not bothered to manufacture such an opportunity. He had, however, obtained the distinct impression that she had been trying hard to amuse her dwindling coterie of long-time admirers, and had subjected her intake of wine to strict rationing. "I'm delighted to find you so cheerful, my darling," he said. "Yes, we shall be saved–I feel it in my old bones. Mephistopheles has been quite a tonic for me, and I feel that I know him more intimately than any other actor has ever had the opportunity to know him."

"You will be magnificent," she assured him, "even if you steel yourself to stick rigidly to Monsieur de Keramour's lines."

"Whatever can you be suggesting, Marianne?" Moineaux countered, feigning shock. "It would hardly be fair to my fellow actors to begin improvising on the first night, would it? Not that I fear that anyone couldn't adapt to it if I did, of course–I have every confidence in my entire company."

"Well, you don't have any significant scenes with me after the end of Act One, so I'll have no need to adapt, will I?" she replied. "You might save any embellishments until your final speech, though. Let Lillette have the chance to settle in as your new leading lady before you start improving Act Two."

"The way things have been going," Moineaux said, with a pretended sigh, "Paul is more likely to embellish his part than I am. He has taken to demonic passion with quite a will. If there's any part of the play that might require improvisation, it's our climatic fight-scene. He's practiced more often with Monsieur de Keramour than with me, and we've never done the scene with the set fully dressed and our costumes fully loaded."

"You've fought on stage so many times before that you're perfectly entitled to assume that you can carry off one more duel without much preparation," Marianne assured him, loyally.

"Perhaps," he agreed. "But this one requires the puncturing of no less than four blood-bags. Since the Grand Guignol has set new standards for the deployment of liquid-filled bladders, the business of killing and dying on stage has acquired new layers of complication. Given that we'll be using steel blades with real points, accurate timing and accurate striking are far more vital than they used to be."

"You'll be brilliant" Marianne assured him. "So will Paul. The one good thing about blood-bags is that, once the first one's burst, the audience is so eager for another to explode that its members become oblivious to false steps."

Moineaux thanked her kindly for her reassurance, and returned to his preparatory labors, in a fervor of anticipation that he had not experienced for many years. He worked like a demon all day, radiating such determined enthusiasm that every member of his troupe was thoroughly infected by it.

Paul Damas lost himself in stern mental preparation, to the point at which he seemed mesmerized, while Lillette Fevret drifted through the empty theater and green room alike as if she were a lovely ghost, distributing ethereal smiles with astonishing grace. Although Marianne became considerably less sober as the early evening wore on, she seemed to be possessed of a wonderful lucidity in the midst of her intoxication, and gathered her own green room following around herself, gaily pretending that the calendar had somehow been set back 20 years.

The anticipated queue did develop outside the box-office as the time approached for the curtain to go up, and Moineaux refused to be dismayed by the dearth of frock-coats and evening gowns. At least, he knew that none of the queue's members had merely slouched around the corner after finding *House Full* notices outside the Grand Guignol; seats for *Les Loups* were freely available to anyone who wanted them.

Alas, Act One did not go as smoothly as anyone had hoped, despite the heroic efforts of its cast to remember their lines and deliver them with appropriate spirit. The fumbles were not very noticeable, but the audience did not seem to be in a forgiving mood. There was a definite increase in excitement when Lillette made her first appearance as the courtesan at the beginning of Act Two, but it died again when she reverted to her other costume immediately thereafter in order to play her crucial scene with Moineaux—who was now Mephistopheles, although Faust's pupil still took him for her tutor.

Moineaux tried with all his might to resist the temptation to embellish his part, but in the end he could not resist cutting a few of Simon de Keramour's more esoteric references and substituting a few light-hearted observations of his own invention, while always being careful to preserve the cues on which Lillette relied.

Lillette was not in the least disconcerted—or even surprised—by Moineaux's slight deviations from the script that they had previously rehearsed, but she stuck religiously to her own scripted lines, and delivered them all with conviction. Moineaux, employing a connoisseur's judgement, thought it the finest scene he had ever seen her play, but the audience did not seem to appreciate it—presumably because they preferred to see her scantily costumed and disporting herself as a personification of lust.

In the interval before Act Three began, Moineaux told his players—honestly enough—that he was very proud of their efforts so far, and that they now had one more golden chance to improve to the level of genius. They signaled their thanks with gestures, and silently expressed their determination to do as they were bid,

With Lillette clad as the courtesan again and Faust at his most energetic, Act Three started well enough, and the audience warmed up measurably. The first duel was effective enough, given that the blood-bags had all been reserved for the second. Germain Querelle and Marianne played a fine scene as co-conspirators endeavoring to cement a firmer union between the rejuvenated Faust and the personification of Lust; then Paul and Lillette took over, bringing the relationship in question to full flower with a nicely-feigned eruption of pure passion.

Meanwhile, Moineaux waited patiently in the wings to make his last entrance, proudly watching his colleagues and pupils justify his faith in them. From where he was standing, the actor-manager only had to move to one side and open a crack between the drawn-back curtain and the proscenium arch to look into the box hovering over the far side of the stage, in which the so-called Simon de Keramour was sitting, but he did not care to do that. He did not want to know, at this point in the proceedings, what the author thought of the performance.

In the box opposite Simon de Keramour's, almost directly above Moineaux's head, the Comte de Farineux would doubtless be leaning forward, switching his gaze back and forth between Lillette and the man he suspected to be his rival for the girl's affections, but Moineaux did not want to know about that either. His only concerns were what was happening on stage, and what effect it was having on the audience.

In artistic terms, he thought that the play had so far been a success, despite the errors that had marred the first act–but he knew that it was not yet the sort of success that would start audiences talking as they departed and make the newspaper reviewers enthusiastic to ply their pens. Its fate still hung in the balance–but he still felt optimistic; he was, at least, prepared to play that role along with his other.

In the privacy of his thoughts, Moineaux began a final rehearsal of the longest of the speeches he would have to deliver after the duel, during which he would no longer have to worry about the possibility of confusing cues that others would have to pick up. He told himself, casually, that it was his duty to improve that crucial speech as much as he could, because there was still too little evidence that the audience was interested in the content of the play rather than its decor. He knew, though, that he had to be very careful in making any amendments on the first night, and would do far better to concentrate on getting the best out of the lines as they were written. He also knew that he would first have to get through his duel with Paul without anything going wrong that would be evident to the audience. He had to make sure that the four blood-bags were punctured in the specified order, each at exactly the right moment, bringing the desired gasp of appreciation from the audience. If the duel went well, the crowd would be in a receptive mood for the final explanatory discourse.

Lillette's final turn as the personification of lust came to its effective end, although she remained on stage to provide a horrified witness to the death of her new lover–her final costume-change, reverting to her student guise in order to hear the end of Mephistopheles' final speech, was a rapid one.

Moineaux counted out the requisite margin following the courtesan's last line, and made his entrance. In the brief dialogue preceding the duel he confined himself entirely to the dictates of Simon de Keramour's script, gathering himself for the action.

For the first time that day, apprehensiveness took hold of him. The duel *had* to be effective. It *had* to rouse the audience to the requisite peak of excitement, so that their arousal might be negotiated into poignancy by his final oration. He *had* to persuade the audience that he really was reclaiming Jean Faust's soul by literally cutting through his flawed cloak of invulnerability. He had memorized the steps of the fight as best he could, and still thought that it would not matter if he had to improvise some of his preliminary passes, but he knew that every move he made had to be effective, maintaining the build-up of excitement. He reminded himself that at least Paul had been schooled to perfection in his own moves. Paul would make no mistakes; everything depended on him–and he was Stéphane Moineaux, who *never* made mistakes.

The wardrobe-mistress had arranged the blood-bags in the suits that he and Paul were to wear with all her considerable skill, and the one that Moineaux was wearing was very snugly accommodated within the sleeve of his waistcoat. Mephistopheles was only required to suffer a tokenistic wound in the arm, while Paul's Faust had three bags secreted about his chemise; he was required to be wounded twice before suffering the fatal thrust to his breast.

As he drew his steel blade, Moineaux allowed himself a slight sigh of regret for the days when it had been sufficient merely to pass a painted wooden blade into the gap between a victim's ribs and arm to signify that he must clutch his breast and pretend to die, but that was his only split second of distraction. Times changed, alas, and he was now in an era of greater bloodshed, to whose methods and ideals he must be fully committed.

The prelude to the actual fight had gone well enough; the audience now seemed to be in a more appreciative mood, and its members were rapt with anticipation of the delights to come. There was a tangible buzz of excitement when the two blades first clashed and the duel got under way with a flurry of blows.

The dance began then; Moineaux and Paul moved about the seemingly-cluttered stage with consummate grace, tipping carefully-prepared obstacles into one another' path, periodically leaping on to the table and the staircase in the finest tradition of theatrical melodrama.

Moineaux relaxed into his role, experiencing the stir of excitement within his own body and the stir of excitement within the audience with equal satisfaction.

When the first of Paul's blood-bags was punctured there were audible gasps from the stalls, even though there could have been few people there who had not seen the trick a dozen times over. There was no such gasp when Moineaux took his own apparent wound, but the air seemed fully charged with expectation. Moineaux felt a fizzing sensation in his nerves and veins that he had not experienced on the Tragicomique's stage for some years. He had to improvise slightly as the fight neared its climax, but the two actors' long experience was standing them in good stead, and the actor-director felt that they were working in perfect harmony. Everything had gone as planned, and it was only necessary to deliver the final sequence of thrusts.

Moineaux looked Paul in the eyes, and Paul met his gaze. The young actor knew better that to let a private smile play on his lips, but Moineaux judged that his *jeune premier* was just as satisfied as he was himself, and that he was relishing the unaccustomed opportunity to die on stage.

As Mephistopheles stood back momentarily, basking in the satisfaction of having inflicted a second apparent wound on his doomed opponent, Moineaux finally permitted himself the briefest of glances at the box where the author was sitting. The actor-manager was delighted to see Monsieur de Keramour leaning forward very avidly, utterly caught up in the spectacle of his labor coming to life for the first time.

Mephistopheles closed in for the kill, as the script required him to do. Moineaux was now following the carefully-prepared directions with the minutest care. He saw Paul position himself to accept the deadly thrust that would penetrate Faust's pretensions, and he moved forward smoothly to deliver it.

Moineaux aimed the climactic thrust with great precision, and lunged forward with a flourish befitting a veteran of five thousands performances on various Parisian stages.

Mephistopheles' face took on an oft-rehearsed smile of triumph.

Paul parried the thrust–which was exactly what the script required him to refrain from doing. Instead of rendering his fatal weakness to the ultimate exploitation, Jean Faust delivered the kind of riposte of which a highly-trained fencer would have been more than proud.

Moineaux saw Paul's eyes flare in alarm and disbelief before he looked down to measure his own fate.

As he saw his adversary's blade sliding between his ribs and into his breast, exactly where the heart ought to be, Sté-phane Moineaux felt another pang of regret for the old days, when a theatrical sword would have snapped rather than vio-late a carefully-prepared script in such an outrageous and ru-inous manner.

He heard Lillette scream, so forcefully that Simon de Keramour would surely be forced to clap his hands over his inadequately-plugged ears. Other screams chimed in with hers, like a complex series of echoes.

Moineaux had just enough time to wonder whether he had somehow forgotten a step, or made an inexplicably gross error of timing, before his mind began to spin.

He felt no pain, but his legs abruptly lost the strength necessary to support him. He collapsed to his knees, and then slumped sideways.

He had just enough presence of mind–or sheer blind in-stinct–to fall in such a manner that the audience could appre-ciate the full tragedy of his demise.

Moineaux did not actually lose consciousness until his head hit the boards of the stage, so he was able to catch one final glimpse of the astonished audience, and sense the shock that traveled backwards from the front row of the stalls, all the way to the tenebrous recesses of the upper circle. They knew it was real. They had seen a great many fights on stage, some designed with the utmost artistry, but they knew that this as real, and that they really might be watching a man die.

12

When Stéphane Moineaux woke up the following morning, he took it for granted at first that he was lying in his own bed, with his head on his own pillow. He had a vague impression that the previous night's performance had gone down very well, and had had a very obvious effect on its audience. It was not until he realized that he could not remember taking his bow that he became conscious of the pain in his chest.

He was astonished that he had contrived to ignore the sensation even for a split second. He tried to move, but immediately decided that it had been a mistake, and resolved to stay very still. He opened his eyes, and tried to measure the dimensions of an unfamiliar room without raising or turning his head.

The scene's backdrop was supplied by neatly-plastered wall brightly painted in a pale shade of blue, bearing two framed monochrome prints set at a parallel height to either side of a gas-lamp. He recognized them both; one was Albrecht Dürer's *The Knight, Death and the Devil*; the other was one of Jacques Callot's illustrations of the second temptation of Saint Anthony. The sunlight illuminating the prints came from the right, where the white-painted frame of a window was visible. The room's doorway was symmetrically placed on the opposite wall. The floorboards were covered by a smooth oilcloth.

Between the bed and the far wall the set was dressed with a night-stand and a scantily-upholstered armchair. A white-clad person of unfashionably short stature stood beside the chair, wearing a stethoscope around his neck like a badge of office. The short man, standing somewhat to the left of center-stage, was leaning towards Moineaux—albeit from a respectful distance—with every appearance of professional concern.

Moineaux had played a dozen physicians in his time, without even counting characters who were actually would-be murderers only pretending to minister to their intended victims, and he knew an unconvincing bedside manner when he saw one.

"Try not to move, Monsieur Moineaux," the physician said. "The blade didn't puncture your heart or your lung, but both organs were forced to move aside as it penetrated the pleural cavity, and both almost certainly sustained slight scratches. The heart, at least, will probably need time to recover before we can be sure that the cut will not open under stress, perhaps fatally. The lesion in the body wall will heal in a matter of days, provided that it doesn't become infected. If either of your internal wounds becomes infected, there is a danger of fatal blood-poisoning. I am Emile Louvois, by the way, lately employed at the Institut Pasteur, but now reassigned to hospital duty."

Moineaux opened his mouth with the intention of giving the incompetent a lecture on the arcane artistry of portraying physicians more convincingly, but even the exercise of his facial muscles seemed, for the moment, to awaken an uncomfortable echo in his breast. All he actually contrived to say, in a whisper so faint that even Simon de Keramour might have had trouble catching the sense of what he said, was: "Am I in Hell?"

"Certainly not." the physician replied, sternly. "As a good positivist, I am bound to inform you that you could not be in Hell even if your wound had been fatal. The mere fact that you can formulate the question is proof enough that you are still alive. If you are fortunate, you will make a full recovery in a fortnight or so. Owing to the unfortunate deterioration of Parisian morals, all the surgeons here have had experience in evaluating and dressing stab-wounds of the kind you have received, and all my colleagues are agreed that your chances of recovery are very good. You must work with us, though, and remain as docile as possible. You shall have the very best of care; the Comte de Farineux instructed that you must have a private room rather than being placed on the ward. I shall allow your visitors to come in one at a time–two, at the most–but I shall give them strict instructions that they are not to disturb or distress you."

"Visitors?" Moineaux queried, weakly.

"There's quite a queue–but if you'll permit me to make a statement on your behalf, the gentlemen of the press will doubtless scurry off to publish what I say. If you're agreeable to my speaking on your behalf, I'll inform them that you're awake and cheerful. I'll tell them, if you wish, that you're hopeful that you'll be back on stage within a month, when you expect Monsieur de Keramour's play to reopen to a full house."

Moineaux wanted to tell the horrid little man that there was no question of the Tragicomique closing its doors, and that the one thing he absolutely must tell the gentlemen of the press was that Monday's performance would go ahead. The other proved, however, to be much better at playing the part of a man in a hurry than he was at playing the part of a concerned physician. He did not wait for the permission he had requested, but rudely turned around and left the room, with a distinct spring in his step that seemed to Moineaux direly inappropriate to the situation.

Moineaux could understand the spring, despite its inappropriateness. It was not every day that a physician who probably spent the bulk of his time using maggots to clean up war-wounds would have the opportunity to tend to a legendary actor. Although his memory was still a little vague, Moineaux suspected that he was first man to have very nearly met his actual end in combat on the Parisian stage for at least seven years.

Moineaux must have dozed off again, or at least fainted as a result of the pain, because his eyes were shut when someone touched his face, after an unmeasurable interval.

He forced his eyelids open, and recognized Marianne Jonquille.

"The others are waiting outside, Stéphane," she said, "but Doctor Louvois said that I ought to come in alone, and that no more than two people were to be let in at the same time under any circumstances. I know you've always hated physicians, but this isn't a good time to indulge your whims—it's best to be a good patient, when you've no alternative. You were very lucky, he says. If the blade had gone in a centimeter to the left or the right, it would surely have pricked your heart more disastrously, or punctured a lung."

She sat down in the chair, having moved it closer to the bedside before waking him.

Moineaux succeeded in formulating a single questioning word: "Newspapers?"

"There were half a dozen reporters outside," she told him, "but they all raced away as soon as Doctor Louvois told them you'd recovered consciousness, to spread the news that you've survived. He told them that there'll be time to issue a correction later if blood poisoning sets in—a trifle tactless, I thought. Or did you mean the morning papers? The doctor forbade me to bring them in, but I've looked at most of them. The reviews aren't actually reviews, of course—they have hardly anything to say about the quality of the play or the acting—but you probably won't mind that, in view of the prominence of the reportage. The tragedy of it all is that we shall be forced to close the theater until you've made a complete recovery. We could have played to full houses for a month and more."

That was too much, and Moineaux knew that he had to find his voice, no matter what price he had to pay in pain. "Are you mad, woman?" he whispered, regretting that he was unable to shout. "Close the theater now and it'll stay closed forever. Absolutely not. Tomorrow's performance goes ahead—and every one thereafter!"

"But we have no understudy ready to play the part!" Marianne objected. "Hubert can't possibly master it in the space of a Sunday, even if we were all to turn out to help him. As things are..."

"Get back to the theater!" Moineaux croaked. "Every damn one of you! Is there one among you who wouldn't kill for an opportunity to play my part, after *this*?"

Marianne shook her head, more in dismay than surprise. "Paul *said* you'd say that," she reported. "He became quite impassioned about it. 'Tonight's audience will forgive Hubert if he's not yet word-perfect,' he said–'and if Hubert shows signs of cowardice, Monsieur Moineaux should simply offer the opportunity to Germain Querelle. Either of them ought to regard a belated chance of glory Heaven-sent,' he declared, 'and Hubert certainly won't want Germain to have it in his stead.' I scolded him, of course–but I didn't tell him what I really thought, which is that he's avid for the play to go on so that he can play his own part again–and to get it right at the second attempt. Imagine–his first opportunity to die on stage and he fluffed it! What a time for force of habit to prevail!"

"Of course he's avid to play his part again," Moineaux whispered. "Quite rightly. Aren't you?"

Marianne had the grace to blush. "Well, perhaps if I were in the lead," she murmured. "Lillette scolded him too, mind– she's very anxious about you. More anxious at any rate, than that damned playwright, who's still complaining that you mis- spoke his lines."

"Wasting time," Moineaux complained, feebly. "Back to theater. Now, damn it!"

"I'll tell them," Marianne said, with a sigh, "but you might have to instruct some of them yourself, if they won't listen to me." She got up slowly and went out unhurriedly.

Almost immediately, Paul Damas rushed in. "I had to come in, *Maître*," he said, "just for a moment. I'm very, *very* sorry–heartbroken. It was an accident, and completely unex- pected. I have no idea what went wrong. The police have in- terviewed me, and are quite satisfied that the blow was not intentional."

"Of course it was an accident, you imbecile," Moineaux retorted, loudly enough to cause his injured chest additional distress. "Just make absolutely certain that Monday's fight comes out the right way. Now *go*! You've got work to do."

Paul went in his turn, but only surrendered his place to Lillette Fevret and Comte Xavier de Farineux.

"Oh, Monsieur Moineaux, it was terrible!" Lillette wailed. "A dreadful thing! Thank God you're all right."

"Fine," Moineaux muttered, through gritted teeth. "Theater. Now."

"I was good, wasn't I?" Lillette went on, relentlessly. "Better than I've ever been before, don't you think? Only tell me that I played my part to my best ability, Monsieur Moineaux, and I'll go back to the theater at all possible speed– but I need to hear it from your lips!"

"Brilliant, m'dear," Moineaux told her, hoarsely. He ran his tongue around he inside of his mouth to moisten his palate, and made a supreme effort to discipline his vocal cords sufficiently to form whole sentences. "There was no finer actress on any stage in Paris last night, Mademoiselle Fevret," he murmured. "Do as well tomorrow, with whoever takes my place, and your days as an *ingénue* are over. You'll be a star."

Lillette seemed delighted with this response, but did not rush to keep her promise.

"You were direly unlucky, Monsieur Moineaux," the Comte de Farineux observed. "I've never seen a man produce a riposte like that on purpose, let alone by accident. At that moment, one could almost believe that the young fool was indeed possessed by devilish passion. When he continued to play his part, you know, I was amazed. You might call it dedication or showmanship, I suppose, but it seemed like macabre callousness to me."

Moineaux had been on the point of letting himself slump into unconsciousness–or, at least, pretending to–but the Comte's last sentence lifted his eyelids with something of a shock. "Play his part?" the actor-manager repeated, speaking a little too loudly for his own comfort. "How could he play his part when he had no more part to play? He was the one who was supposed to die. The play's remaining lines belonged to myself, with some trivial support from Lillette and Marianne."

"The women were no help at all," the Comte opined. "Not to Monsieur Damas, at any rate–I couldn't see whether they were able to do anything for you. The stage-hands brought the curtain down as soon as they saw that you were hurt, but Monsieur Damas stepped smoothly out on to the forestage as it fell, and delivered a final speech. Whether he was apologizing in his capacity as an actor or improvising some sort of discourse in his guise as the demonic Faust, I can't say. I wasn't really paying attention to what he said, for I was more than a trifle distracted by seeing what had happened to you. I was convinced at first that the blow was mortal. Whatever he said, though, the remainder of the audience seemed to take it well enough."

"In fairness," Lillette said, "you had set a precedent for improvisation yourself, when you were playing your scene with me in Act Two. You inspired us all with your improvement of Mephistopheles' philosophy. Even so, I never knew that Paul had it in him to make up a speech–if that's really what he did. As Monsieur le Comte says, he may simply have been apologizing to the audience for the play's premature conclusion. I wasn't listening either–I was frightened that you might be dead."

"I didn't know he had it in him either," the Comte's added, supportively. "The boy always seemed a trifle stupid to me, but perhaps it's the parts you give him. If he made a speech up on the spur of the moment, it was damnably astute of him. I dare say you'd have been proud of him, Monsieur Moineaux–almost as proud as I am of my darling Lillette."

"I must have trained him very well indeed" Moineaux whispered, not certain whether to believe it. "What on Earth did he say, I wonder? What did the author think of his improvisation?"

"I have no idea what Monsieur de Keramour thought," the Comte said, a trifle frostily, "and I've no intention of asking."

"I haven't had a chance to talk to him," Lillette said. "He wasn't outside in the corridor just now, though he surely ought to have been. Do you really think that I was brilliant, Monsieur Moineaux? As good as Sarah Bernhardt, do you think?"

Moineaux let his eyes fall shut again, and wished that it required more of his once-legendary artistry to play the part of a man whose strength had been utterly sapped by pain and exertion.

"Go," he whispered. "Theater. Now. Can't see anyone else today. Tell everyone–play your hearts out tomorrow, for me! Make Monday's performance magnificent!"

Lillette, able to recognize a commanding cue when she heard one, blew him a kiss and turned to make her exit.

The Comte followed her–but he looked back as he reached the threshold. "I still can't remember a single word of what the boy said no matter how hard I try," he confessed, "but to judge from the audience reaction, anyone who was there last night might reckon the true ending weak by comparison with whatever young Damas did."

The Comte closed the door behind him. He and Lillette had evidently taken note of Moineaux's penultimate instruction, for no one else came in to replace them.

Instead of allowing himself to lapse immediately into unconsciousness, Moineaux furrowed his brow. *If Paul can remember his improvisation well enough to do a command performance*, he thought, *I'll have him repeat it at my bedside next time he comes to visit. But it won't be as good as the substitute speech on which I was working. That really would have given the audience something to think about.* As he drifted off into a tortuous dream, though, he could not help remembering his brief dalliance with the notion that *Le Nouveau Faust* might work better if Mephistopheles had repossessed his own physical form as soon as his final sword-thrust had sent Jean Faust to damnation, and delivered his final judgement on the human condition from the mouth of the younger actor, in a tone resonant with strange regret.

13

That sabbath was the most uncomfortable of Stéphane Moineaux's life, not so much because of the pain of his wound–although that was considerable–as because of his helplessness to assist in the preparations for the most important performance ever to take place at the Tragicomique.

Despite the restlessness provoked by the latter circumstance, the intensity of the pain in his chest diminished by slow degrees. Having lost its sharpness, though, it seemed to enter into an unholy collaboration with his other torment, taking on the quality of an unscratchable itch that was all the more irritating for its relative quietness. He fretted and fidgeted all day long in dire anxiety, not for fear of the blood-poisoning that might yet condemn him to death but because he was so desperately curious to know what was happening at the theater.

Had Hubert Marin accepted the responsibility of stepping into his shoes? Assuming that were so, would the old hack be able to learn all the words in time? Would Paul and Simon de Keramour be able to teach the lumbering ox the steps and moves of the climactic fight scene? Most importantly of all, would the newspapers give sufficient prominence to the information that the second performance of *Le Nouveau Faust* would take place as advertised, even though the Tragicomique's courageous actor-manager was badly injured and might die at any moment? Would the reporters give sufficient emphasis to the assertion that the play's cast wanted nothing more than to offer up a suitable tribute to the spirit and endurance of their father-figure?

Sisters of Mercy came in occasionally to check his dressing, but Moineaux was not grateful for their attentions, whose kindness retained a censorious element. Although they dressed in absurd costumes and played conscientious roles themselves, nuns had a tendency to disapprove of more versatile actors, with the result that one of the few vocations the actor-manager trusted even less than that of physician was that of bride of Christ.

Emile Louvois called in on him twice more in order to pronounce himself satisfied with his patient's progress, but informed his patient on each occasion that no one had sent any news from the Theater. He volunteered to discuss the implications of the quashing of Alfred Dreyfus' conviction instead, but Moineaux had far more important things on his mind than the honor of the French military establishment or the fate of the luckless officer.

By the time darkness fell in the world outside, Moineaux had begun to identify very sympathetically with the light of Callot's print, no matter how difficult it was for him to imagine himself as a saint. One of the nuns eventually brought in a nightlight, explaining to him that the hospital's gaslight was for the use of the physicians and surgeons, not the patients, and that the gas-lamp in his room would only be lit if Doctor Louvois required brighter illumination than the candle in the nightlight could provide.

With the aid of a draught of laudanum, Moineaux slept deeply enough that night, but his sleep was by no means peaceful. Indeed, the drug seemed to increase the vividness of his dreams, which seemed so frightful while he was experiencing them that he was quite amazed when he discovered, ten or 15 minutes after taking a meager breakfast on Monday morning, that he had forgotten every detail of their terrifying contents. Was that a merciful release, he wondered, or an extra dimension of irony belatedly added to their harassment of his imagination? The breakfast helped him feel better, though, and he did not have much difficulty in sitting up to partake of it. He was allowed to read a newspaper, although he threw it aside as soon as he had ascertained that the evening's performance at the Tragicomique had indeed been advertised, in an almost-satisfactory manner.

A police inspector came in to question him at 11 a.m., even though he had given Doctor Louvois strict instructions that he did not want to see anyone at all until 11 p.m., when the performance at the Tragicomique would be complete and he would be more than willing to receive news of it. Moineaux sent the fellow away with a flea in his ear.

"Paul Damas is a son to me!" he said, hurting himself with his own vehemence. "The accident was entirely my fault–my own stupid clumsy fault. Arrest me for criminal negligence if you must, but let the boy alone. I forbid you to pursue him any further, even if I should die. He has a part to play tonight–and for many nights thereafter, come what may."

The doctor had the grace to seek his permission before disobeying instructions for a second time in the late afternoon, and Moineaux relented when he was told that the visitor asking to see him was the Comte de Farineux.

"How are things at the theater, sire?" he asked, as soon as the hero of the Second Empire had sat down, "How are the rehearsals going?"

"I'm afraid I don't know yet, Monsieur Moineaux," the Comte replied. "I'm on my way there now, but I thought I'd best stop off to find out how you are, so that I can answer the inevitable questions in the green room. Lillette made me buy all the Sunday newspapers yesterday, mind. You'd think from the eulogies that you were dead already–perhaps it's the modern fashion to get the obituaries out in advance. How are you feeling, my dear fellow?"

Moineaux pursed his lips in frustration. "Do you remember the adaptation of *Le Juif Errant* we staged last year, sire?" he asked.

"Certainly," the Comte replied lifting a quizzical eyebrow.

"Do you remember the scene in which Rodin, suffering from the cholera, claps a red-hot poker to his breast, in order to burn out the fever?"

"I never believed it would work," the Comte opined. "Oh, I see–you're attempting to draw a colorful comparison. In your situation, old chap, I'd probably excuse myself from maintaining that sort of act for a while–there's no need to strive for eloquence while you're laid up with a wound, and probably no point in the attempt. For future reference, though, I've been pricked more than once by a sword, and I've had more than one wound cauterized on the battlefield. The two sensations are not at all alike, you know. That's the trouble with actors, if you'll forgive my saying so–they lack experience of life."

"Thank you, sire," Moineaux murmured. "I'll try to remember, for future reference, that the comparison in question is empirically invalid." He reminded himself that it was the Comte who had paid for him to be placed in a private room, but gratitude did not prevent him from reflecting that there were times when Monsieur de Farineux and his once-lovely sister offered convincing evidence of the validity of the principle of heredity.

"I invited Madame de Vernier to come with me to visit you," the Comte said, as if he had somehow caught a telepathic echo of Moineaux's uncharitable thought. "She's far too busy, alas–but she asked me to give you her very best wishes for a speedy recovery."

"Please thank her kindly for me, sire, and assure her that I'm not in the least put out," Moineaux said.

"Lillette will doubtless demand that I bring her to see you after the performance," the Comte went on, "but I don't think it's a good idea. You'll be enthusiastic to hear news, of course, but Monsieur de Keramour's rig is so much faster than mine, thanks to those excellent horses of his. He's certain to want to bring you intelligence of the performance without delay. Young Damas will insist, if he shows a moment's reluctance."

"To see Paul or Marianne will be quite enough, Monsieur de Farineux," Moineaux assured him. "Too many visitors all at once might be stressful."

"That's what I thought," the Comte said. "You must concentrate on getting your strength back. Monsieur Marin will doubtless be a woefully inadequate substitute for your artistry–the audience will miss you terribly, but they'll forgive your understudy any clumsiness, because their thoughts will be with you. People are very eager to see the play now. That ridiculous little man was hammering at the box office door like a madman last night, as soon as you'd been carried out on a stretcher, demanding to reserve 21 tickets for the night of your return performance, whenever that might be."

"What ridiculous little man?" Moineaux asked, wondering whether he had lost track of the conversation due to his own mental confusion or the Comte's tendency to ramble.

"The one in bicycle shorts I recklessly invited to my Hôtel after you advertised him last year as an up-and-coming genius."

"Jarry? *Jarry* reserved an entire row of tickets for the night of my return performance?"

"Quite–he's mad as a hatter, in my opinion, but I suppose his heart's in the right place. It must have been some kind of flamboyant gesture of solidarity between gentlemen of the theater. How things have changed since the old days, eh, Monsieur Moineaux? He wasn't alone, mind."

"Do you mean that *other* people wanted to reserve 21 tickets for my return performance."

"No, of course not–I mean that other people wanted to buy advance tickets one or two at a time, even before this morning's newspapers published advertisements saying that the performances would continue. You're a success again, Monsieur Moineaux–as you fully deserve to be, having gone to such extraordinary lengths to please the crowd. I'm sorry– that was tasteless. I want to reassure you, by the way, that I wouldn't dream of trying to find Lillette a position at the Gambardi or the Bouffée while you're ill. You have my full support, as well as that of your company. Eventually, I suppose, she'll be looking for something at the Ambigu or the Gymnase, or somewhere even better–a starring role, of course–but in the meantime, she's very happy at the Tragico-mique. You need have no worries on that score."

"I'm grateful for your reassurance, Comte," Moineaux said–slightly absent-mindedly, because he was still grappling with the implications of the Comte's earlier statements. He was too late to stop his runaway mouth adding: "I'm sure that Monsieur de Keramour will be equally delighted."

"I still don't have the faintest idea who that fellow is, you know," the Comte remarked, generously refusing to notice the tactlessness of the remark. "My friends tried their hardest to make conversation with him on Thursday last, you know–I asked them to make him welcome for politeness' sake–but they told me that he's devilishly difficult to talk to. Seems incapable of answering an innocent question. No one in Paris knows anything about him, so far as I can tell."

"Paris is not the world, Monsieur de Farineux," Moineaux said, doing his best once again to play the part of a man on the brink of falling unconscious. "We Parisians like to think so, of course–but I suppose we must accept the fact that there are many living people, including Frenchmen, who have never been to Paris in their lives, and who are totally unknown to everyone in the city."

For once, the Comte picked up on Moineaux's gathering desperation, and took the hint that the conversation ought to be cut short. "You're obviously exhausted, old man," he said. "I'd better be getting on. I'll tell the green room crowd that you're as well as can be expected, and that you send them all your very best wishes. Since you've asked me not to, I won't come and see you again after the performance, even if Lillette begs me to bring her. She'll just have to be content with me telling her how brilliant she was, for a change." With that, he picked up his hat and stick, and went to the door.

14

When Moineaux opened his eyes again, the little night-light had been brought in, although the last rays of twilight had not yet faded away and a pale grey light still crept through the window to add an extra dimension of sinister grotesquerie to the Dürer and the Callot. Doctor Louvois was taking his pulse–a procedure that evidently did not require gaslight.

"What time is it?" Moineaux asked, abruptly.

"Nine o'clock," the physician replied. "You're making good progress, Monsieur Moineaux. Not a trace of fever as yet. I'm optimistic. We have a great deal for which to thank Messieurs Pasteur and Metchnikoff, you know. They have wrought a revolution in medicine comparable to the one that Monsieur Lavoisier contrived in chemistry before the deluded idiots of the Convention sent him to the guillotine."

"A matter for great regret," Moineaux murmured, "as I tried to make clear the night before last, in my capacity as a contrite Mephistopheles."

Louvois could not have understood the reference, but he knew who Mephistopheles was. "As a good Comtean," he said, earnestly, "I can't approve of superstitious nonsense, even in the popular theater. The arts should take a lead, in my opinion, in driving obsolete nonsense out of the public con-sciousness, rather than striving so hard to maintain and nour-ish it."

"You sound more like a Platonist," Moineaux observed, "intent on driving artists out of the ideal Republic into the wilderness, lest they disturb the sacred quest for calm of mind. Except, of course, that Plato was being ironic. Your taste in decoration is a little odd, I think, if you are really trying to extirpate all superstition." His gaze flickered in the direction of the prints on the far wall.

"If I had my way," the good Comtean assured him, "I'd get rid of those. I'd replace the Dürer with one of the artist's excellent anatomical studies, and the Callot with a photomicrograph of a disease bacillus, taken with the aid of one of the new generation of microscopes, manufactured since the problem of chromatic aberration was solved. There's the real ultimate enemy of humankind, Monsieur Moineaux: the bacillus."

"I'm sure that a clear sight of the enemy would inspire patients to recovery, Doctor Louvois, even in the absence of eyes with visible whites," Moineaux said, with only a modest trace of irony. "It is always useful to have the measure of one's adversary, and to know the range of his capabilities. In the meantime, however, the humble bacillus supplies you with your living and your status in society; were science to discover a meaning of its extirpation, you'd be as redundant as a poet in a Platonic Republic. Do you not sometimes feel that you have entered into a sort of Faustian bargain with the demonic microbial host?"

"Please don't try that argument on the Sisters," Louvois said. "It's hard enough for a positivist to work with devoutly religious assistants without such intrusions–which helps to prove my point. It's high time the legendary Faust was left to his damnation, as a silly relic of anti-scientific prejudice, rather than being continually fêted in all manner of melodramas."

"Ours is one of many new Fausts," Moineaux murmured. "Whatever the writer of the *Faustbuch* intended, the Fausts of the 19th century are heroes, not fools. Monsieur de Keramour's allegory favors science rather than opposing it."

"I understand the case you're attempting to make," the doctor said, "even though I haven't seen your play. Faust has become a symbol of sorts for the whole of civilized humankind, forsaking an obsolete religion based on brazen moral terrorism for a new empire of Reason and Enlightenment. I understand why you believe that beneficiaries of scientific progress have every justification for being proud of him–but still, as a Comtean I am bound to favor plain speaking and seeing things for exactly what they are. The Medieval Church needed allegory to obscure the many contradictions in its beliefs and teachings. The champions of positivism do not, for science is coherent as well as empirically justifiable. Your play is a relic of obsolete procedure as well as obsolete thinking, Monsieur Moineaux."

"Thank you for your advice, doctor," Moineaux murmured. "I suppose, since the Comteans have invented humanist churches in which men may worship the redundancy of God, they might as well go on to devise theaters in which men may excite themselves with the absence of melodrama. Monsieur de Keramour, my worthy playwright, assures me that the Chevalier de Lamarck was once able to enrapture audiences with the idea of evolution, and Monsieur Flammarion seems well able to do the same with the wonders of binary stars and the canals of Mars. Even so, I shall cling to my conviction that there is still a role for drama to play in human affairs, even at the level of Grand Guignol horrors. You must come to see my Mephistopheles when I am able to return to work, doctor–you might like him better than you imagine."

"If the rewards of theoretical and mechanical progress really were the Devil's gifts," Louvois said–having wrinkled his nose at the mention of Camille Flammarion's name, on the grounds that the astronomer was even more famous as a spiritualist than he was as a popularizer of science–"then we would be morally bound to thank the Devil for his clarification, and curse God for having withheld such nutritious fruit for so long–but that is unnecessary. The truth, Monsieur Moineaux, is that the rewards of theoretical and mechanical progress are a purely human achievement; *that* is what we should recognize and celebrate in our modern mythology. We should discard the entire imaginative apparatus of silly superstition within our literature and replace it with a better one: a clear-sighted apparatus that has no truck with such bugbears as Mephistopheles. You will forgive me my little outburst, I hope–it's a subject about which I feel strongly."

"There's nothing to forgive," Moineaux assured him, in a whisper. "You have a point, and every right to chide me if you suspect me of corrupting the morals of the young–although I'd be grateful if you didn't medicate me with hemlock. I still think you might like the play, though. Monsieur de Keramour's demonic Faust is a strange hybrid, and so is his humanized Mephistopheles; no good positivist could approve of either if they are taken too literally, but the truth is as fully entitled to benefit from every rhetorical device as the most seductive lie. Art that provokes philosophical contemplation and cultivates poignant responses should be admired and treasured, doctor, not despised and discarded."

"Don't tire yourself out with passion, Monsieur Moineaux," the doctor advised. "I'm sure that we'll have plenty of opportunity to discuss such matters coolly in the future."

Moineaux obeyed the injunction, so far as audible speech was concerned, but he could not help his mind running on a little way. *Had Paul's Faust only been content to lie down and die, as he was required to do*, he thought, *my Mephistopheles could have delivered a discourse recognizing and celebrating human achievement of which any true scientist–which is to say, any scientist possessed of imagination and versatility of thought–could have approved thoroughly. Perhaps that is the direction in which I should be trying to move the speech.*

Remembrance of the fact that Paul's Faust had *not* been content to lie down and die, however, soon sent his thoughts off at a tangent, and he drifted off into a reverie, assisted by the eerie quality of the nightlight's illumination.

"I wonder," he murmured, aloud, "exactly what Paul did say to the audience, when the performance was so unexpectedly and dramatically interrupted. What would I have done, had I been in his situation? I really don't know. Is it possible that Paul pretended that the exchange of identities had been reversed at the conclusion of the duel, so that he could speak as Mephistopheles and not as Faust, thus enabling him to draw upon the provisions of the script to conclude the play? Surely not. It's far more likely that he issued a simple apology for having to end the performance prematurely–but if so, why did the Comte de Farineux get the impression that the audience liked what he said? I wish I had asked him about it when I saw him–although, of course, I couldn't, because I didn't know what he'd done until after I'd sent him away."

He assumed, while he muttered all this, that he was alone–but he was not. The doctor had not left the room, and was still standing beside the bed, studying his patient despite the gloom, with a contemplative finger pressed to his mouth. He moved that finger now to say: "Don't trouble your mind with too much cogitation either, Monsieur Moineaux. That will certainly invite delirium. The mind needs relaxation just as the body does, in my opinion. If you can keep a clear and serene head wile you're awake, you'll sleep far more peacefully. It would be easier if you were a committed positivist, of course, but an actor ought to have the mental discipline to hold himself together. You must take a dose of laudanum now–you need a good night's sleep."

"To Hell with your sedative, doctor," Moineaux said, having remembered all of a sudden why he disliked physicians so much. "I seem to have been sleeping most of the day, although I'm damned if I can keep track of the time. I have to stay awake now, at least until midnight. I need to know how the performance went, if I'm to have the slightest chance of sleeping peacefully. When can I get out of here to watch a performance for myself? Tomorrow, do you think?"

"Certainly not," said the scandalized Louvois. "I might consider sending you home at the end of the week–by which time you should be safe from infection, if no symptoms have developed–but when I say home, I mean *home*. I absolutely forbid you to go near the Théâtre Tragicomique for a least a fortnight. You must rest, Monsieur Moineaux, in order to let the healing process run its course. If you were a younger man, you might perhaps be up and about in ten days, but you're not–and I strongly advise you to take the sedative."

"Go away, please," Moineaux said, only stopping himself with difficulty from replacing the word *please* with something along the lines of *you thrice-accursed quack*. "If I need rest, I'll do what I can to rest–but I'll only have peace of mind when I know that everything's going smoothly at the Tragicomique. As soon as someone–anyone–comes from the theater, you're to bring them in, whether it's Paul, Marianne, or Hubert... bring them all in, if they all come. I need to know that all's well, or I'll be in agony all night, whether I'm conscious or unconscious."

"Oh, very well," said Emile Louvois, with a sigh. "You can stay awake for a while longer. I'll bring your visitor in as soon as he or she arrives–assuming that anyone does arrive. Try to lie quiet until then."

Moineaux did his best to obey that final instruction, despite the increase Doctor Louvois had brought about in his dislike of physicians–but his good behavior went entirely unrewarded.

When the doctor finally came back, some time after the nearest church bell had chimed midnight, he was alone. He brought a fresh nightlight with him, to replace the one that had guttered out some little while before.

"I thought it best to tell you the news myself, Monsieur Moineaux," the physician said. "I must insist that you take some laudanum first. You'll have plenty of time to hear what I have to say before you go to sleep."

Moineaux cursed the scoundrel roundly this time, but in the end he had to agree to the doctor's terms. He was not yet strong enough to get out of bed, knock the irritating fellow down and make his way to the nearest cab-stand.

"Well," the actor-manager said, when he had downed the draught of medicine that Doctor Louvois had prepared. "Did the performance go smoothly? Is everyone happy with the way it turned out?"

"Far from it, I fear," the doctor reported, with the flatness of tone appropriate to the sober reportage of a good positivist. "There was an accident in the final act almost identical to the one that struck you down. I say *almost* because the blade went straight through Monsieur Marin's heart. He is dead, and Monsieur Damas has been arrested for culpable homicide."

Moineaux made every effort to rise up and strangle the physician, but his wound was still too painful and the dose of laudanum he had taken proved to be well-measured. He fell back senseless, without inflicting any damage at all.

His dreams that night were perfectly frightful.

15

Moineaux usually forgot his dreams and nightmares almost as soon as he woke up, despite making frequent determined efforts to salvage whatever imagery he could, just in case it might be good raw material for dramatic development. When he did contrive to preserve something, the images were always too incoherent and too personal to be of any use.

When he woke on the morning after hearing news of Hubert Marin's death, however, the nightmares would not let him alone for some considerable time. Their torment extended into his waking moments with savage brutality. Had he wanted to capture and preserve any of them for future reference he could have done it with ease–and he would not have been in the least intimidated by their frightful quality. Alas, for all their vividness, the images were just as idiotic and senseless as ever; he was ashamed of having entertained them, even while he was robbed of the power of conscious reason.

If I were a more accomplished dreamer, he thought, *I'd have spent the night engaged in a sharp duel of wits with God and all the saints, in the character of Faust or Mephistopheles or some chimerical combination of the two. It seems that my sleeping self is not enough of a positivist, or not enough of an actor, to cut such gaudy metaphysical cloth into any kind of neat pattern.*

He was able to sit up for breakfast again, and almost managed to convince himself that he had mastered and banished his pain, but he was fidgeting far more fretfully than he had the previous day when Marianne Jonquille finally arrived to confirm and add detail to everything that Louvois had told him in summary.

Hubert Marin had played the part of Faust-turned-Mephistopheles with mind-numbing mediocrity, until the moment when he was supposed to kill the rejuvenated Faust—at which point Paul Damas' riposte, though clumsier by far than the one he had produced on the opening night, had found the understudy's heavy-larded torso too tempting a target. The blade had slipped between Marin's ribs and ripped into the left ventricle of his heart; the poor fellow had died in less than a minute, leaving the Tragicomique's stage liberally stained with real blood.

While the understudy's body was being removed, however, Paul Damas had apparently stepped in front of the precipitously-fallen curtain for a second time, and had delivered another improvised speech—or perhaps the same one, with further embellishments. The only thing of which Marianne was certain was that Paul had spoken at considerably greater length and apparently with greater conviction than he had on the Saturday night.

"I couldn't concentrate on his words, I fear," the actress said, apologetically. "My thoughts were all for poor Hubert. The audience applauded wildly, though—I've never heard such clapping. I didn't take a bow—nobody did, except for Paul. Perhaps it was unwise of him to seem so composed, although I'm sure that he must have been in turmoil inwardly. The police arrested him while he was still on stage, and the applause increased in volume even further when they did it, although I don't know whether the audience thought that the arrest was part of his performance. They took him away to prison—when I find out where he's being held, I'll go to see him, if they'll let me in."

For the first time in years, Marianne's sobriety was very conspicuous. It was not simply that she had not taken a drink since before the previous night's performance, in Moineaux's estimation. What had happened to Hubert had knocked some-

116

thing out of her. Her face was grey and haggard; the color of her once-beautiful green eyes seemed to have faded to an ochreous yellow. Her present sobriety was no mere absence of intoxication; it was something deadening, anaesthetic if not actually toxic.

"No," Moineaux croaked, having carelessly omitted to moisten his mouth. "There's no time for that. You have to take command, my love. You'll have to prepare *two* actors for to-night's performance. Germain will have to take my part, and Fernand must play Paul's. They'll have to be replaced in their turn, but the company's large enough—you won't have to draft any scene-shifters to play the trivial parts, although I dare say they'd be glad if you did."

"Are you mad, Stéphane?" Marianne retorted. "We can't possibly go on tonight."

"You must," Moineaux said. "If Germain won't do it, I'll come myself. If I have to play the whole part sitting down, including the duel, I'll do it. Whatever the cost, the play has to go on."

"We can't, *Maître*," the actress insisted. "We simply can't. The newspapers are raving about the theater being cursed, and the police have applied to the censor to have the play closed down. No official order's been issued yet, but it's surely only a matter of time. It's over, Stéphane. You have to accept that."

"Never." Moineaux struggled to prop himself up on his elbow, and succeeded. From there, he assumed, it was only a matter of continued effort to sit up properly, swing his legs over the side of the bed, and stand up. All he needed was a few seconds' rest...

The few seconds had become a full minute when his plan was interrupted. There was a brisk knock on the door, and Simon de Keramour came in, wearing his smoked lenses and equipped with earplugs.

"*Maître*," the playwright said, without any sort of polite preamble, "I need your authority to take command of the Tragicomique. You must name me as your surrogate, with

117

Madame Jonquille as a witness, in order that I can instruct the company to make ready for tonight's performance."

"This is madness!" Marianne protested, again. "In any case, Monsieur de Keramour, if anyone ought to inherit Monsieur Moineaux's mantle of authority, it should be me. I tell you plainly that there is no way that the Tragicomique can continue to stage your play. That need not distress you overmuch—it has created a greater scandal in its first two days than all the Grand Guignol's productions of the last two years. You're famous now, Monsieur de Keramour, and every theater manager in Paris will be begging you to let him produce your play. You can name your own price and your own cast. For the moment, though, you must go away, lest you complete the work of killing this poor man."

"No!" Moineaux gasped. "The closure of the theater would kill me, but Death shall not have me while it remains open. While there's life in the Tragicomique, I refuse to let it die."

"Don't be a fool, Stéphane," Marianne instructed him, sharply. "Monsieur de Keramour can't keep the theater open against the censor's order. If he appeals the decision, he should be able to persuade the authorities, once everything has settled down, that his play was not to blame for Hubert's death, and that it can and should be staged again, albeit with wooden swords equipped with proper buttons."

"You're behind the times, Madame Jonquille," Simon de Keramour told her. "The censor has made his decision, and has refused the demand to close the production. He's a devout follower of Auguste Comte, it seems, and cannot tolerate any talk of curses. He considers it beneath the dignity of his office to pander to vile superstition, and he has stated firmly that since there is nothing in the play that warrants its suppression on moral or political grounds, it shall not be suppressed."

Marianne was obviously taken aback by this development, but she was not yet defeated. "In that case," she said, "you'll have no trouble at all staging it elsewhere. It is clearly in your interest to do so. You have lost both your leading actors, and there is no audience in the world that will respond kindly to a production in which two exceptionally demanding leading parts are taken by Germain Querelle and Fernand Cornu, without the benefit of proper rehearsal. This farce is over, Monsieur de Keramour, and I would like you to leave me alone with my friend, so that I might comfort him and do what I can to assist in nursing him back to health."

Had he been able to, Moineaux would have let loose a "No!" that would have blasted the roof off the hospital and made the towers of Notre-Dame vibrate in sympathy. As it was, the syllable was only a little more powerful than a jackdaw's caw–but it did make the two combatants turn their attention to him, with grave concern in their eyes.

"You're killing him!" Marianne complained.

"On the contrary–I'm trying to save his life!" Simon de Keramour retorted.

"I shall save his life, and his theater," Marianne Jonquille declared, striking a pose reminiscent of her glory days. "I am a woman, I know, but we are living in the era of Sarah Bernhardt and Loie Fuller, and no one can sensibly claim that a woman is incapable of directing a theater by virtue of her sex. I know how the Tragicomique runs far better than anyone else, and I can manage it better than anyone else. More importantly, I know every one of Monsieur Moineaux's creditors, and I know exactly how to persuade them to give us the extra time we need to recover from this crisis. The publicity we have had will guarantee our future, even if we do not open again for a month–and Monsieur Moineaux's return to the stage will be a great event. Alfred Jarry has bought 21 tickets for the occasion, with the intention of distributing them to every French writer of note who cares to accept the gift–and who will refuse him, in the circumstances? We do not need your play, Monsieur de Keramour, although I shall of course be delighted to make a new contract with you if you will only consent to wait until Monsieur Moineaux is fully recovered. I must insist, however, that I, not you, must be entrusted with the role of his legal representative–and I demand, Stéphane, that you make that appointment now, with Monsieur de Keramour as our witness."

Moineaux let his head fall back on to his pillow, and he stared up at the ceiling. *The newspapers are foolish*, he thought, *to start prattling about a curse after two coincidental accidents. The Tragicomique has a proud record, despite the recent decline in its fortunes. Anyway, we're living in a positivist era, and rumored curses no longer deter anyone from anything. Quite the reverse, in fact. Publicity like that is worth its weight in gold.*

In the meantime, the argument went on.

"I have no wish to suspend the performance of my play, Madame Jonquille," Simon de Keramour went on, in a more moderate tone than before. "I have no wish to take it to another theater. Monsieur Moineaux was kind enough to give me a chance, and I have no intention of deserting him in his hour of need. I want to stage *Le Nouveau Faust* tonight, at the Tragicomique, and I would be delighted if you would consent to continue playing your part. Please, Monsieur Moineaux– give me the authority to command your company, and I shall make it happen."

"You can't," Marianne said, flatly. "You can order Germain and Fernand to take the parts, if Stéphane is foolish enough to give your permission, but that doesn't mean they'll be able to play them with anything resembling competence."

"I have no intention of casting Germain Querelle and Fernand Cornu as Faust and Mephistopheles," de Keramour replied, with the air of a man producing the ace of trumps at a vital point in a game of whist. "I have two other players ready and willing to take the parts."

Moineaux raised his head again at that, and licked his lips.

"Who?" demanded Marianne, stridently.

"Who?" whispered Moineaux, like a bizarre echo.

"I shall play Paul Damas' part myself," the author announced, portentously–and then paused, like a true melodramatist, for effect.

"What about mine?" Moineaux whispered, resignedly supplying the cue.

"Your part, *Maître*," said Simon de Keramour, "will be played by a man who has no fear whatsoever of any curse or accidental mishap, having once been the finest swordsman in France: the Comte de Farineux."

"What?" cried Marianne Jonquille. "You can't be serious."

"Indeed I am," the author said, smugly. "He has seen the play twice, with two different men playing a scene of the utmost poignancy opposite his beloved mistress. Marin, he says, was an utter disaster in the role–although I must say, *en passant*, that he stuck more closely to my lines than you did, Monsieur Moineaux–but he seems to have found your own performance rather inspiring. He says that he would have auditioned yesterday, if he had been able to learn his lines in time. This morning, he swears that he is ready–and Lillette, who has been rehearsing with him, concurs."

"Madness!" opined Marianne.

Moineaux had to agree with her, up to a point–but he knew that madness, like curses, was nowadays a tradable commodity whose value was perversely on the rise. How would the newspaper-reading public react to the news that the Comte de Farineux, hero of the Second Empire, was to stand in for the two men who had been struck down in the climax of Simon de Farineux's play? It might be better, of course, if he were able to face Paul Damas rather than a substitute–but as substitutes went, the play's author was little short of ideal, even if his passionate feelings for Lillette were left out of account. Tonight's performance would have been guaranteed abundant newspaper coverage in any case, but a performance with Comte Xavier de Farineux playing the philosophically-transfigured Mephistopheles, fighting a duel against an author who would finally have the opportunity to guarantee that his play would conclude as it had been written rather than with some actor-improvised fudge, would attract enormous attention. No one would care overmuch about the quality of the

121

individual performances–the mere fact that the play was being staged would be an unprecedented sensation.

Simon de Keramour must have thought that Moineaux was hesitating over the matter of giving him the authority he had requested, for he went on: "Tonight's performance was sold out before last night's, but I have heard of tickets changing hands for as much as 1000 francs–with the proviso that the performance goes ahead, of course. Nothing like this has ever been seen before, in Paris or anywhere else in the world. I don't ask you to let me take over your theater, Monsieur Moineaux–indeed, I'd be exceedingly grateful to Madame Jonquille if she would consent to take over every responsibility save for the direction of the play itself–but if the play is to go on tonight, then I must direct and play in it."

"Agreed," whispered the stricken actor-manager.

"No!" Marianne protested.

"Yes," Moineaux said, as firmly as he could. "If you will not bear witness to the agreement, call Louvois. The performance will go ahead, just as Monsieur de Keramour has planned. I wish that I could be there–and if I find myself able to stand up at six o'clock, I shall be. But please, Monsieur de Keramour, I beg you–do your utmost not to hurt the Chevalier. A long time has passed since the battle of Sedan left us bereft of heroes, and Xavier de Farineux is a national treasure of sorts. He really is very fond of our dear Lillette. I would not want him to hurt you either, so–*no pointed blades*. If you can puncture the blood-bags in some other way, all well and good, but if not, set them aside. You *must* use weakened weapons, with blunted ends, so that any accidental blow will break the instrument and not the skin."

"We shall use foils equipped with buttons," Simon de Keramour assured him. "I had already decided on that. Fake blood is a superfluity, in my opinion, if not a distraction; we shall do without it tonight."

"Then you have my full authority, and my earnest blessing," Moineaux said. "You must play your part, Marianne, if you want to retain my good opinion. I beg you to do everything possible to assist Monsieur de Keramour."

Marianne looked like a woman who had just been reminded, very forcibly, exactly why she had avoided sobriety for such a long time. "As you wish, *Maître*," she said, eventually.

16

Moineaux tried to go back to sleep then, but he could not do it–or thought he could not, at any rate. The daylight streaming through the window seemed uncommonly bright–as it certainly was, by comparison with the feeble nightlight with which he had been provided–and the actor-manager felt a pang of sympathy for Simon de Keramour's hypersensitivity.

Instead of drifting off to sleep, Moineaux dreamed while he was apparently still awake that a subtle but dire infection was slowly taking hold in the slight wound on the surface of his heart, and was commencing the cunning work of leaking poison slowly into the ventricle, from which it was conveyed into his arteries and then his veins. He became convinced that this crawling chaos would consume him eventually, but he also remained certain that it would give him time to see one last performance at the Tragicomique–if not tonight, then tomorrow.

He was able to eat a light lunch, though, and Doctor Louvois told him that all the surgical staff of his hospital were delighted with his progress.

"It is another victory for Pasteur, Metchnikoff and the genius of the modern pharmacopoeia!" Louvois declared, deliberately posing himself like an old-fashioned tragedian. "Positivism triumphs again!"

Lillette Fevret came to see Moineaux that afternoon, without her watchful cavalier in attendance. The Comte was very busy at the theater, she said. He had instructed her to return there with all possible haste, although she felt that her own part was exceedingly well-prepared, and that his greatest need was to rehearse the duel scene very religiously, until both the combatants were certain that no further mistake could possibly be made.

"I needed to get away for a breath of fresh air," the ex-*ingénue* explained, "and I wanted desperately to see how you are. Everyone is avid for news. It will give them all such heart for tonight's performance if I can take good news back to the green room."

"I'm getting better, though not as rapidly as I could wish," Moineaux assured her. "Even the doctor thinks so–and physicians are not always wrong, thank God."

"I'm very glad to hear it," Lillette told him, "and everyone else will be as glad as me."

"I wish I could be there," Moineaux said, with absolute honesty. "It was very foolish of me to let this happen. I should have known better, given all my years of experience. What a fool I was!"

"Not at all," Lillette assured him, generously. "You could not have anticipated what would happen. If anyone was at fault, it was Paul, although I'm perfectly certain that he would rather have been stabbed himself than kill poor Hubert. The police have arrested him, but it's ridiculous to think that he might have done it on purpose. They'll have to release him, won't they, Monsieur Moineaux? The Comte would have contrived his release by now, I'm certain, if he hadn't been so busy–I'm sure he'd rather go on opposite Paul than Simon. Simon's not an actor, after all, and he's going to look slightly ridiculous playing a Faust who has supposedly been made invulnerable to all mortal ills while wearing protective lenses and earplugs."

"I'm sure that Simon will do his very best," Moineaux said, automatically, "and that the Comte will be well content

124

to play opposite him." *Especially in the final duel*, he thought, but did not voice aloud. He hurried on to say: "And I'm sure that you'll be as brilliant tonight as you were last night. Marianne and Simon both sang your praises when I saw them this morning."

"I *was* quite good last night," the ex-*ingénue* assured her employer, "even though Monsieur Marin was every bit as terrible as they say. He certainly didn't deserve to die, of course, but if he had been a better actor he'd surely have done what you contrived to do, and taken his heart out of the way."

"Is there any news of Paul?" Moineaux asked. "Do you know where they've taken him, and whether an investigating magistrate has been appointed to evaluate the case?"

"I've heard no news as yet," she said, "but I'm sure he'll be all right. It would be good, wouldn't it, if he were able to return to his role when you return to yours?"

"Yes, my love," Moineaux said. "That would be very satisfactory. With luck, though, he'll be back on stage before me."

"I ought to go now," Lillette told him, "but I'm glad I was able to come to see you. Everyone misses you terribly, but I miss you even more than the others. I'll be more delighted than you can imagine when we're able to play our scenes together again–especially the one in which I'm Faust's pupil, who doesn't realize that you're no longer Faust but Mephistopheles."

"You're very kind, my dear," Moineaux said. "I'm sure that your visit has speeded up my recovery considerably. Give my good wishes to everyone–and be brilliant. Remember that you're the play's star, and by far the best actor in it."

He expected no more news that afternoon, but no more than an hour had passed since Lillette's departure when more news came, brought by Paul Damas.

"The investigating magistrate is fully persuaded that it was another accident," Paul explained. "Like the censor, he will have no truck with talk of curses, and he understands that I have no possible motive for wanting to hurt you or Monsieur

Marin. The public prosecutor is still entitled to bring a charge against me if he wishes, but in the absence of a supportive instruction, it's unlikely to succeed in court. I've been released until a formal decision is made–unfortunately, I've been prohibited from playing my part at tonight's performance. I've appealed against the decision, on the grounds that it's nonsensical, but I won't have an answer until tomorrow at the earliest. I'm truly sorry, *Maître*."

"It's not your fault," Moineaux assured him. "The Comte will be a catastrophe in my role, of course, and I doubt that Monsieur de Keramour will do any better in yours, but at least they'll move Heaven and Earth to ensure that there won't be any more accidents. They'll stop the gap until you're given permission by the court to return to your role, and I defy my doctors in order to retake mine. What a sensation our return will be, my friend! If we're fortunate enough to be able to return on the same night, I'll show you what a fluke your stroke was; I'll kill you with all the flamboyance I can muster."

"I shall be delighted to let you kill me, *Maître*," Paul replied, with all apparent sincerity, "and I shall die with equal flamboyance. You have no idea what a strain it was improvising those final speeches. I suspect that whatever I said was entirely different on the second night from the first, but I really can't be sure, for I can't remember a word of what I said on either occasion. I know that I only intended to apologize to the audience for having to stop the play short of its conclusion, but my head was whirling, and I'm sure that I said far more than I initially planned to, last night especially."

Moineaux frowned at this revelation, which seemed to him as ominous as it was strange. "That's a great pity," he said, "for I'd dearly like to know how you satisfied the audience–and how you saved the plot of the play from mere suspension or dissolution into chaos, if that's really what you did. If we can't find anyone in the cast who was paying attention, we'll have to find someone who was in the audience to tell us what you said. Are you quite certain that you can't remember any of it?"

"Not a word," Paul confirmed, regretfully. "It was pure instinct–or demonic possession. Thank God that Monsieur de Keramour won't be forced to any such necessity. He, I suppose, will be just as glad to die as I shall be, since it will allow his own ending finally to be manifest upon the stage, presented in an orderly manner, exactly as the script commands. Whatever got into me will hopefully find him a much tougher nut to crack–unless, of course, it actually was the Devil."

There was a moment's awkward silence then, before Moineaux said: "You're too much a product of your era to mean that, Paul. You may not be a positivist, like the argumentative Doctor Louvois, but you don't believe in the Devil."

"I didn't," Paul confirmed, "until last night. The first time, I was able to tell myself that it really was an accident–some kind of random twinge that happened to have direly unfortunate consequences–but I couldn't do that a second time. Last night, I was very conscious of the possibility that something might go wrong, and was trying my utmost to ensure that it didn't. We're always saying that we do things despite ourselves, but that's just a way of speaking. Last night, though, the sword in my hand really did kill Hubert Marin in spite of my making every possible effort to ensure that no such thing could happen. It was no mere slip, *Maître*, although I'm glad that I convinced the investigating magistrate that it was. Hubert's death was no accident. Whatever took control of my arm took aim with deadly accuracy. If it wasn't the Devil, *Maître*, what on Earth was it?"

"I don't know," Moineaux confessed, uneasily. "But I refuse to believe in the Devil, or in curses."

"If curses have to be cast," Paul said, soberly, "then I can't imagine who could or would do such a thing. It's not just the *what* I can't figure out but the *why*. What motive could anyone, or any*thing*, have for doing what it did? Why injure you? Why kill Hubert? Why go so far as to introduce a pause into the laws of physics, to severely injure one innocent man and kill another, merely to sabotage a play?"

"The fact that there's no conceivable reason probably implies that there was no such motive involved," Moineaux opined. "Except that..." He stopped abruptly.

"Except what, Monsieur Moineaux?" Paul asked, after a slight pause.

"Except nothing, I was merely about to observe that the play hasn't actually been sabotaged. It will play to full houses until well into the next century, wherever it's staged."

"So you think that Simon..."

"No," Moineaux said, firmly. "That's exactly what I can't and don't think, and why I said *except nothing*. If Simon de Keramour had that sort of power, he'd find a much simpler way to ensure his play's success. If he were the Devil in disguise, he wouldn't have to stoop to such silly trickery."

"If he were the victim of trickery rather than the perpetrator..." Paul said, tentatively. "If he were more akin to Faust than Mephistopheles..."

"If he'd sold his soul to the Devil to guarantee his play's success," Moineaux told him. "He wouldn't have needed me. He'd have taken it to the Ambigu, or the Opéra–and he'd have been as careful to put a safety clause into the Devil's contract as he was to put one into mine. No, Paul, no matter how disconcerting your double experience was, it wasn't the result of diabolism, or any kind of curse. You'd do better to consult Charcot at the Salpêtrière than search out an exorcist."

"So you think it *was* my fault?" Paul riposted.

"No, I don't, "Moineaux insisted. "I know you, Paul, and I know how distressed you must be–but the investigating magistrate is right; however bizarre it may seem, the sequence of events really was a chapter of accidents. You mustn't begin to think that you're Devil-led, Paul. I've heard it said that the Devil's greatest weapon is that people refuse to believe in him, but it's the opposite that's true. The only power the Devil retains is the force of people's belief in him, and you mustn't grant a foolish idea the authority to hurt you. You haven't done anything wrong, and you're no more a victim of some evil supernatural entity than I am."

"The latter part of that argument isn't exactly reassuring," Paul pointed out.

"It was badly phrased," Moineaux admitted. "You're not the victim of some evil supernatural entity, Paul. Nor am I. Given time, we'll prove that. For now, we have no alternative but to be patient."

Paul nodded his head, and deliberately looked away in order to collect himself. "An odd choice of decoration," he observed, nodding in the direction of the Callot.

"True," Moineaux conceded. "All things considered, though, I'd rather have that on my wall than a vastly-magnified image of a bacillus, or a detailed picture of a dissected limb. Positivism has its darker side, just as the Gothic imagination has."

"Wherever you turn," Paul murmured, "you just can't win. And it isn't Jean Faust or Mephistopheles saying that–it's me."

Act Three
Monsieur Moineaux's Comeback

17

The rest of the day proved somewhat more comfortable
for Moineaux than either of its predecessors. The gradually
fading pain of the wound in his breast had passed through its
irritating phase and was now no more than a dull ache, as long
as he did not move too abruptly. The ferment in his mind
seemed to have undergone a similar process of evolution;
sharp and vexatious anxiety had similarly given way to a dull
sensation that was much closer to resignation than desperation.

So much had happened in the previous 48 hours that the
mere continuance of the chain of circumstance now seemed to
constitute a victory of sorts–the only sort of victory that currently seemed imaginable. Moineaux had tried to get out of
bed at six o'clock, and had actually managed to stand up, but
he knew that any attempt to make the journey to the Théâtre
Tragicomique would set him back considerably, while another
day's patient recuperation might leave him much better able to
discharge himself from the hospital on the following afternoon. There would be time enough to see his company perform with its two new leading men, and it would probably be a
great favor to his own theatrical sensibilities to give the Comte
and the playwright a little more time to practice their roles.

There was no sign of Doctor Louvois in the early evening, but the dutiful nuns attended to his trivial needs. The Sister who brought his nightlight in–again before the twilight had
entirely faded away–reassured him that another 24 hours
would see him past the critical point at which internal infection might reveal itself in pain and fever. He slept a little, but
as 11 p.m. approached he became increasing wakeful and ex-
pectant. He determined that he would not take any sedative

dose that night, but would instead make every attempt to prepare himself mentally and physically for an early return to
work. The candle in the nightlight went out again, but the sky
outside must have been cloudless, for the starlight falling on
Callot's harassed Saint Anthony was quite adequate to display
the poor man's anxious face.

This time, it was a little before midnight when Doctor
Louvois came in bearing a fresh nightlight. The positivist
made no attempt to bargain with him, and did not even seem
to have any laudanum about his person. "Monsieur de Keramour is here to see you," the physician said, in a voice whose
quality was difficult to evaluate. "He's brought news from the
Tragicomique."

"I've been expecting him," Moineaux told the doctor.
"Please show him in."

"I really ought to give you a sedative first," the doctor
said, but it was merely a token gesture; he had anticipated refusal and consented in advance.

"I'm feeling much better this evening," Moineaux assured him. "I believe that I shall sleep quite well, once I know
that all is well at the Tragicomique. Show Monsieur de Keramour in." As he spoke, though, his observation of the doctor's
expression caused his brows to knit; there appeared to be
something that the physician was very conspicuously not telling him—something that had upset the man.

He had already guessed what the truth must be when
Simon de Keramour barged past the doctor into the room, his
face a mask of horror. The playwright was not wearing his
smoked lenses, but his eyes were no longer blue; indeed, the
irises seemed to have swollen in dimension, and to have
turned jet black. For half a second, Moineaux wondered
whether the Breton might indeed be possessed by the Devil.

"It was an accident!" the playwright cried, at a volume
that must surely have hurt his seemingly-unshielded ears. "An
unaccountable accident! Three doctors all gave the same
opinion—death by natural causes! It wasn't my fault, Monsieur
Moineaux. I swear that it wasn't my fault."

"Who's dead?" Moineaux asked–not because he was in any doubt, but simply because he needed to hear the name spoken aloud.

"The Comte de Farineux," the playwright confirmed.

"When?"

"At precisely the same moment as the other accidents–but my mock-weapon shattered in my hand, Monsieur Moineaux. The buttoned tip did not so much as scratch his waistcoat. I saw it in his eyes, *Maître*! I saw in his eyes that something was horribly wrong. Were it not absurd, I would declare that he died of fright!"

"It is possible to die of fright," Doctor Louvois put in. "It's not just a theatrical *cliché*. A severe alarm can stop the heart. Fear born of superstitious belief is a terrible affliction."

"It seems improbable that the Comte died of superstitious anxiety or stage-fright," Moineaux observed, surprised by his own calmness. "If he believed in curses, he believed even more firmly in his ability to defy them–and had he suffered from fatal stage-fright, he'd surely have perished before the performance began or during Act One. To get all the way through to the end of Act Three seems far more suggestive of the possibility that he over-exerted himself in the course of the pretended duel. He was no longer a young man, and he gave up fencing practice a long time ago." While he spoke, though, he continued staring at Simon de Keramour's night-black eyes, wondering what sort of affliction could have caused such an alarming symptom.

The playwright was obviously uncomfortably aware of the same phenomenon, for he muttered an apology as he sat down, leaned deeply forward, and reached up, almost as if he were about to pluck the offending organs from his head. When he straightened himself up again, though, his eyes were bright blue. There were two black circles resting in the palm of his hand.

"I've heard of that invention!" Louvois exclaimed, excitedly. "Lenses placed in direct contact with the eyeball–but I never hard of them being manufactured in black glass."

"I could hardly play the part of a supposedly-invulnerable man in smoke spectacles," Simon de Keramour explained. "I had to adopt less obtrusive measures. My ears are still ringing a little, I fear, despite the laudanum I took to dull their sensibility."

"You played your part while drugged?" Moineaux queried. *And why not?* he thought, *Marianne often plays her parts drunk.*

"It's not just newspaper reporters who are talking about a curse now, Monsieur Moineaux" Simon de Keramour said, wearily. "Everyone's talking in those terms. One accident is mere happenstance, while two can be accounted as coincidence, but three... and you did not see his eyes, Monsieur Moineaux. You did not see his eyes."

But he must have looked into yours, Moineaux thought, wondering whether the playwright had bothered to tell his fellow players about his ingenious new method of protecting his sensitivity. Aloud, he stated firmly: "There is no curse on the Théâtre Tragicomique, I have owned it and worked there for nearly 20 years, and..."

"And that's exactly what some of the rumor-mongers are saying," the playwright told him. "They've deduced that the curse came into being when you were hurt on Saturday night, and they claim that anyone who attempts to play your part in your stead will likely perish. That party is competing, of course, with the one whose members claim that it's my play that's cursed, or me–but the one thing no one is saying out there on the streets is that talk of men being killed by curses is ludicrous."

"Perhaps it's as well that we have Monsieur Louvois with us," Moineaux said. "As an ardent champion of positivism, he will doubtless assure us that belief in curses is a product of nonsensical superstition, unworthy even of a journalist."

"Your confidence in me is heartening," the physician replied, "and I am happy to oblige you. Belief in curses *is* mere superstition, unworthy of the credence of any devotee of reason–but I would need to be convinced that the Comte de Farineux qualified as a devotee of reason before I could declare that a curse could not kill him. Belief in the power of curses, you see, might be mortal in itself, in the right circumstances. If what Monsieur de Keramour says about the Comte's eyes can be taken seriously, then it might have been a sort of fright that stopped his heart."

Moineaux was perversely pleased to hear the physician echo what he had said to Paul Damas earlier in the day about the Devil's power being rooted in mistaken belief, but he was convinced that there was a different argument applicable here. "What Monsieur de Farineux believed," he insisted, "more than any other item of faith, is that he was a great swordsman. He cannot possibly have taken alarm at the thought of dueling a playwright-turned-actor armed with a fake weapon designed to break at the slightest strain. I could not call him a Comtean, but he was certainly a reasonable man by the standards of the day. He could not have been convinced that there was a curse on the theater, or the play, on the basis of what happened to poor Hubert or anything that he saw on the Tragicomique's stage."

"Nevertheless," said Simon de Keramour, "I am sure that he was frightened by something–or, if not frightened, seized by some very similar emotional shock."

"Perhaps, Monsieur de Keramour," the physician suggested, "you are confusing the cause and the effect. Perhaps it was his consciousness of the fact that all was not well with his heart that frightened him."

"You did not see his face, Monsieur," the playwright said. "I did–and I tell you that there is not a man in France who will consent to play that part in tomorrow's performance."

"As to that, Monsieur de Keramour," Moineaux told him, confidently, "you're quite wrong. If I'm any judge of men, every old soldier of the Second Empire who still lives will blow the dust off his scabbard tonight and polish his sword, with a view to taking the Comte de Farineux's place and avenging his honor. There'll be a queue outside the theater before dawn. If your play were really in need of fodder for its curse, it would have a supply adequate to last out the year, even before bravos began arriving from Italy, *matamores* from Spain and Regency bucks from England, every one of them anxious to demonstrate that he has whatever it might take to break the curse. Not that we'll need them, of course, for the so-called curse won't last until the weekend, let alone Christmas."

"I would willingly take to the stage myself," Doctor Louvois declared, "to fight against an alleged curse for the honor of positivism."

"That won't be necessary, doctor," Moineaux assured him. "Might I ask you to leave me alone with Monsieur de Keramour now? We have certain confidential matters to discuss."

The physician was evidently less than delighted with this request, but seemed unable to think of a reason to deny it. "I'm on duty all night," he said, as he performed a conspicuously slight bow before withdrawing. "If you need me, you have only to ring. Please don't worry about your expenses, Monsieur Moineaux. I'm perfectly happy for you to continue to occupy a private room, despite your guarantor's passing."

"That potential problem had not occurred to me," Moineaux admitted. "Thank you for your consideration, doctor–and goodnight."

18

When the doctor had closed the door behind him, Moineaux tried to sit up in bed, and contrived to raise himself up without suffering any significant pain. "Sit down, Monsieur de Keramour," he said.

The playwright sat down. "Are you really proposing to keep the theater open and the play running?" he asked.

"Certainly," Moineaux told him. "We must seize our victory with both hands, and claim the triumph that is our due. If tickets for tonight's performance were selling for 1000 francs, what must tomorrow night's be worth? We won't be the only ones crying 'The show must go on!' If the censor were to change his mind now and attempt to close the show down, there would be riots in the Place de la Concorde. We're making history here, my friend—and we'll continue to make it for as long as we can. Not that I want to see anyone else die, of course—but we ought to be able to prevent that from happening easily enough, whether or not we can figure out exactly what did happen to the poor Comte. You must be very impatient now to see the ending of your play come out the way it's supposed to. What did you do, by the way, when the Comte collapsed? Did you drop to your knees beside his body and lament the tragedy, or did you step on to the forestage and make a concluding speech?"

"I did step forward as the curtain came down," the playwright admitted. He was looking at Moineaux quizzically now, as if he were uncertain what direction the actor-manager's train of thought had taken. His eyes seemed unnaturally huge, now that the pupils had shrunk to pinpricks again, and the yellow candlelight had turned their bold blue color to a sly turquoise.

"Do you remember what you said to the audience?" Moineaux asked.

"No, I don't. It was pure instinct, I'm afraid. Had I known what Paul Damas had said to conclude either of the previous performances, I'd probably have followed his example. Perhaps I did—but my mind was just as full of confusion tonight as it had been on the previous occasions. The laudanum I'd taken before the performance probably didn't help my clarity of mind. I honestly have no idea what I said."

"And have you any idea why you killed the Comte de Farineux?"

"But I didn't!"

"Not literally, perhaps–but in the context of the play, that's exactly what you did. The riposte with which Paul struck me and Hubert Marin is not in the script, and Paul–who had been very carefully rehearsed, thanks to you–should not have made it. Indeed, the Comte himself assured me that he should not have been able to make it, even if he had intended to. If there is anyone who has an obvious interest in making the duel come out correctly, Monsieur de Keramour, it's you– and yet you, who knew every step of that routine as well as Paul did, nevertheless made that same impossible riposte against one of the finest swordsmen France has ever seen. If anything frightened the Comte de Farineux to death, it was that. Your sword shattered, and the button hardly scuffed the Comte's padded waistcoat–but how on Earth did you come to make the stroke in the first place? And how on Earth did you steer it past the Comte's guard?"

Simon de Keramour was silent for half a minute before he said: "I don't know. I had no conscious intention of doing it, and I have no idea how the trick was worked."

"You don't know what got into you?"

"No."

"But something did *get into you*, didn't it? Something made that stroke, which wasn't you."

"I can see why you sent the doctor away," de Keramour retorted, after another pause. "A good positivist wouldn't like what you're suggesting."

"Not necessarily," Moineaux countered. "You've already heard him say that although he doesn't believe in the power of curses, he does believe in the power of belief in curses. I agree with him. I don't believe in the power of demonic possession, but I do believe in the power of belief–or, more specifically, in the power of theatrical illusion. I don't believe that a play- wright, no matter how obscure and mysterious his background might be, could actually *be* either partner in a diabolical pact, in any sense beyond the trivially metaphorical, but I certainly believe that an actor playing a part can occasionally lose him- self in that part."

137

"Two actors," Simon de Keramour pointed out, "in three different performances. But we didn't lose ourselves in the part–quite the reverse. Because of what we did, the part was irredeemably lost."

"In fact, there were four actors involved," Moineaux said, by way of correction. "Five, if you include me. Furthermore, there's a great deal of difference between losing oneself in a part and following a script–but that's not the point we need to address. The important thing is that we're clearly not dealing with random events here, Monsieur de Keramour. The three sword-strokes weren't like three distinct spins of a roulette wheel. The fact that an accident happened once made it more likely that a second one would occur, and the fact that a second did occur increased the likelihood of a third mishap considerably."

"Why?" the playwright asked.

"Because we're dealing with human actions, not mere matters of chance. We're dealing with the vagaries of the human mind–and lone of the most fundamental aspects of mind is an inclination to search for patterns, often discovering apparent instances that have no true basis in reality. A roulette wheel has no memory, but the mind has; when the wheel has come up red five times in a row, it remains just as likely that it will come up red again–but you'll never find a man who'll bet that way, even if he knows full well that the chances remain even. The hunger for patterns, and the insistence on finding them and believing in them, even in the manifest absence of any logical association, is what superstition *is*–and none of us is free of it, or ever can be. It's a by-product of reason itself: a natural consequence of the conviction that there's an order in nature that can be detected and articulated, in order that we can anticipate the outcomes of known situations."

The playwright furrowed his brow as he tried to digest the implications of Moineaux's argument. "So, when you say that *something got into me* when I made that riposte," he said, eventually, "you're not implying that I really am a stand-in for Faust or Mephistopheles, or that I was momentarily possessed by some other evil spirit, but rather that I was somehow tricked by my own mental processes into following a pattern I'd perceived, even though I was consciously committed to doing the opposite?"

"Exactly," Moineaux confirmed. "Mind you, I can't be absolutely certain. I might be more confident if knew what was in the speech."

"Which speech?"

"The speech that whatever *got into* you and Paul made after the curtain came down: the speech that started as an apology but might have gone on to provide some sort of substitute ending for your play. The speech that no one remembers... no one, that is, in the cast of the play. One person, at least, must have heard it clearly enough, and understood its significance."

"Who?"

"Alfred Jarry. He's a fellow playwright, who was sitting in the audience on the play's first night, and who immediately went out and hammered on the box-office, demanding 21 tickets... but not for the following night's performance, oddly enough. It was Paul who delivered the speech on that first occasion, but it was my return performance for which Jarry demanded his 21 tickets."

"Why would anyone buy 21 tickets?" de Keramour wanted to know.

"I'm not sure–about the number, that is. Perhaps that's all he could pay for with the money in his possession. As to the purpose of the purchase, though, Marianne says that he intends to distribute them to discerning friends and fellow writers. That appears to be in character–and even Jarry shows some consistency of character, despite the fact that it runs directly contrary to his aesthetic convictions."

"I can't imagine why he, or anyone else, would do such a thing," the playwright finally confessed, "and I have no idea why you think the fact significant."

"Jarry believes that the theater needs shaking up," Moineaux told him. "He disapproves of plays that pander to the audience's aesthetic expectations, especially in the matter of imposing a stereotypical moral order on the pattern of events represented within a play. He disagrees violently with the principle of poetic justice, which claims that because the author of a play has the power to determine that good actions will be rewarded and evil ones punished, he also has a moral responsibility to contrive such an outcome."

"But a tragedy..." Simon de Keramour began.

"Is only a subsidiary variation," Moineaux told him. "The sense of tragedy generated by a play whose hero dies is entirely dependent on an audience's expectation that poetic justice will prevail. The same is true of the ironic component of the kind of *conte cruel* that figures large in the Grand Guignol's productions. Monsieur Jarry disapproves of conventional tragedy just as much as he disapproves of conventional happy endings and conventional examples of the irony of fate. He does, however, approve of the more barbaric aspects of melodrama. He believes that the best goal of theatrical performance is to shock an audience out of its moral and aesthetic complacency by manifesting the unexpected, forcing its members to entertain ideas they had never admitted into their heads before. He approved thoroughly of Méténier's use of a blood-bag in *Mademoiselle Fifi*, but was dismayed when the device became an instant theatrical *cliché*. I suspect that he loved the ending forced on *Le Nouveau Faust* by my misfortune on the first night precisely because it wasn't an ending–or, if it was, because it was the kind of ending that could only be contrived by an actor's hasty and unrehearsed improvisation. He couldn't have known then, of course, that the accident would be repeated twice more on successive nights; he must have expected the play to revert to its script in my absence. He had enough confidence in my directorial flair, however, to believe–or at least to hope–that when I was able to return to work I might take advantage of the opportunity that chance had thrown my way, and mould the play in consequence."

"You mean," Simon de Keramour said, his tone mingling shock and disgust "that this impudent oaf expected you to embrace the chaos precipitated by your accident, and alter *my* play in response?"

"Why not?" Moineaux countered. "Isn't that exactly what *you* did, last night, despite your own intentions and ambitions?"

The playwright was rendered speechless by that observation.

"I did tell you, the first time I met you, that your play needed work," Moineaux reminded him, after a brief interval. "I had tried to rework the ending myself in advance of the opening night–privately, since you were so determined not to discuss any possible changes–but I confess that I hadn't yet considered anything as radical as the improvisation forced by the accident–although I suppose, in retrospect, that it's exactly the kind of narrative move that Jarry might have made. I did think, at one time, that the last speech ought to be Faust's rather than Mephistopheles'–or, that if Mephistopheles is to be granted his regretful final judgment on Faustian ambition, then he ought not to be in Faust's body when he delivers it–but I let my egotism overrule my judgement in both cases, because it seemed that both options would give the last word to Paul Damas rather than myself. My accident seems to have overruled my judgement on that score, albeit in a rather crude fashion."

"You have no right to rewrite my play," Simon de Keramour stated, grimly. "I am the one who decided how it would end, and the only one who can determine any changes. I was very careful to have that included in the contract we signed."

"So you were," Moineaux agreed. "But there appears to have been an unforeseen flaw in the bargain, does there not?–a flaw that even you were powerless to repair, when the crucial moment arrived. Auguste Comte's devoted followers could not possibly approve of the suggestion that some supernatural agency is determined to rewrite your play, and I dare say that they would be equally dissatisfied if I were to suggest that your play might be struggling to rewrite itself–and yet, your play *has* been rewritten, at every single one of its performances, perhaps not identically, but at least along the same general lines. You may be its author, but even you could not prevent yourself making the unscripted riposte that precipitated its variant ending. How delighted, do you think, would Jarry be with *that*?"

Simon de Keramour was silent for more than a minute. "But you don't suspect any active supernatural agency?" he said, finally. That seemed to Moineaux to be a distinctly evasive response.

"I don't feel entitled, in the year 1899, to speak in those terms," he admitted, "but something is happening here, Monsieur de Keramour, that neither of us understands. The linguistic terms we select in order to describe it are less important than the fact itself–and the question of what we intend to do about it."

Again the playwright hesitated for a long time. Eventually, he said: "I have not, to my knowledge, made any pact with the Devil," he said. "I have made something of a mystery of myself, it's true–but that's mere performance. It doesn't hide any sinister secret. I really am a Breton, from an old family, which fell on hard times long ago. The only reason I have for not telling you my real name is that you wouldn't recognize it–it would mean less to you than *de Keramour*, which at least preserves an echo of the melodramatic tradition in which you work."

"For what it may be worth," Moineaux said, "I too have not knowingly made any pact with the Devil. Not literally, at any rate. I had an interesting conversation with Doctor Louvois a little while ago in which we agreed that Faust is nowadays symbolic of all civilized humankind. In 1899, he is Everyman, to the extent that there can any longer be an Everyman. We representatives of western civilization have all cultivated secular knowledge of the world, even if we have conserved faith alongside it–and to set such knowledge alongside faith is, indeed, tantamount to shunting God aside, and placing an adversary on His throne. That is why the world still has room for, and perhaps a need for, yet another new *Faust*.

That is why we should be prepared to wonder what, if the whole human world is Faustian, we ought to make of Mephistopheles, our tempter and betrayer. As I said before, though, the terms we use to discuss these things are less important than the brute fact that confronts us, and the formulation of our plan of action. I mean, of course, the brute fact that we have a lethal play on our hands, and must plan to do something about it other than—or, at least, as well as—exploiting the commercial opportunity that its lethality presents."

"Can we make such a plan, in the time available to us?" Simon de Keramour said.

"Of course we can. I already have—do you think I've been idle while I've been lying here waiting for my wound to heal? Am I not Stéphane Moineaux, the greatest actor-manager in Paris? Don't answer that—I couldn't bear to hear you agree that I am Stéphane Moineaux and then say no more. But we shall need a full cast to put the first phase of my plan into operation. Will Marianne be fit to go on tomorrow do you think?"

"As fit as she ever is," Simon de Keramour replied, cruelly. "Drunk or sober, it will make little difference to her performance."

"What about Lillette? How badly has she taken the Comte's death?"

"Not as badly as she pretends, if my judgement can be trusted. She is staying with Marianne tonight, and will doubtless be wearing black in the green room tomorrow, but she knows full well what she was to the Comte, and he to her. Her grief is no deeper than her make-up."

"You are a trifle uncharitable, I think—but probably right. Good. Have you any notion as to whether Paul will be allowed to play?"

"Paul is unnecessary. I shall play his part—but who will replace de Farineux as my counterpart? Even if you're correct in your judgement that there will be a thousand amateurs enthusiastic to pit their swordsmanship against the curse of the Tragicomique, or Devil himself, I doubt that you could find

143

one among them capable of learning the part in less than a day,"

"The audience won't be there for the actor's performance," Moineaux said, reflectively. "You must select one, and rehearse him, in case my first plan goes awry. The prompter will doubtless have to work very hard, if he actually has to play the part, but from the viewpoint of the audience, Acts One and Two will be pure tantalization, merely forcing them to a torment of impatience. When the climax of Act Three arrives, they'll be on more excruciating tenterhooks than any theater audience in history, even if you have to go on with an amateur. But that's a contingency plan–with luck, it won't be necessary to put your man on stage at all."

Simon de Keramour nodded his head slowly, obviously having caught up with Moineaux's train of thought. "You won't make a fortune out of this, you know," he said. "Tickets might be selling for thousands or tens of thousands on the street, but you sold them all out of your box office at face value.

"No, I won't make a fortune," Moineaux admitted. "Not immediately, at any rate–but the members of my company will know their worth as they play their parts, won't they? They'll know what I've made of them, and I'll know what I've made of myself. If I contrive to come through this, I'll soon be able to pay off all my creditors and begin to store up a nice nest-egg for my retirement. If not... well, I'll make a spectacular exit."

"Would that really be worth dying for?" de Keramour asked, soberly.

"I've died 3000 times at least for a pittance and a smattering of grudging applause," Moineaux told him. "I'll have to do it in actuality some day, and will only do it once–it would be pleasant, don't you think, to have the entire population of Paris, and a substantial fraction of the provinces, on the edges of their seats while I take the risk?"

"The doctor won't let you out," de Keramour predicted. "Not tomorrow night, or the night after."

"I don't intend asking his permission," Moineaux told him. "We'll need the understudy, though, just in case the doctor turns out to be right and I fall down dead before I even get to the stage door. Go home and get some sleep, Monsieur de Keramour–and tomorrow, get to work early. Send a note round to Jarry, by the way, telling him that I plan to be there, if it's humanly possible. You'll find his address in the book in my office. If all goes well, You must also hire an amanuensis. Install him in your box, or in the wings, or in some other convenient corner, and give him firm instructions to record every single word of the play's final speech, no matter who makes it. I'll see you at the theater shortly before the performance is due to begin, If I'm not there, start without me."

"I don't believe the Devil himself could stop you getting there," de Keramour opined, "whether he'll let you leave the stage alive might be another matter. I don't want to kill you, *Maître*. I don't even want to lend an arm to something that might."

"You won't," Moineaux told him, wishing that he could be more convinced of that certainty himself. "I've already told you–I have a plan, and it has far more to it than a mere determination to turn up and say my lines. It's a crazy plan–but in a crazy situation, what other kind of plan can possibly work?"

"Will you tell me what it is?" the playwright asked, narrowing his eyes against the feeble candlelight.

"Certainly not," Moineaux told him. "We're involved in a melodrama, after all–surprise may not be everything, but it's not to be despised. Don't worry. If my plan works out right, you'll be in no more danger of dying than I am."

"Given your present condition," Simon de Keramour observed, "That cannot qualify as a reassurance."

"It was badly phrased," Moineaux admitted. "If my plan works out right, we shall both survive. Will that do?"

"I suppose it will have to," the playwright conceded, having already conceded, tacitly if not explicitly, that the play must go on no matter what, and that Moineaux must take back his part if he could actually contrive to get to the theater.

19

Moineaux received only one visitor the next day, although his physician, with his permission, turned away several others that he did not wish to see.

Doctor Louvois did not know what the actor-director and his playwright had talked about, or what they had agreed, but he had returned once Simon de Keramour had left and had claimed to be able to detect obvious signs of strain in his patient once the interview was over.

The doctor prescribed absolute rest for the following day, and seemed quite adamant in his determination to stand guard over Moineaux's door like a dragon guarding a hoard of treasure. He could doubtless have turned back the Garde des Sceaux or the censor with perfect ease; there was, however, one force of persuasion against which neither he nor his patient, being mere mortal man, could possibly prevail.

When Lillette Fevret came into his room Moineaux could not help smiling, even though she was dressed in mourning and moved to the chair as if the weight of the world had descended upon her shoulders. When she had dismissed the doctor, however, and heard the door close behind him, Lillette threw back her veil and looked at Moineaux very frankly, with eyes that were quite untroubled by tears.

"I'm sorry, *Maître*, but I had to see you," she said. "I confess freely that I didn't come here for your sake, but for my own. If you tell me to go away, I will. I don't wish to submit you to the least inconvenience."

"I'm delighted to see you, my dear," Moineaux assured her. "In serving your own ends, you will doubtless lift my spirits considerably. Please remain as long as you wish–but you do intend appearing in tonight's performance, I hope?"

"I wouldn't miss it for the world," Lillette assured him. "The Comte's sister will think it inappropriate, I know, and there will be many among her friends who will feign indignation, but they know full well what our relationship really was. I don't need to continue my performance of grief here, do I, *Maître*?"

"No, you don't," Moineaux assured her. "You're a consummate actress, my dear–far more obviously so in the green room and at the Hôtel de Farineux than I have so far allowed you to be on stage, but you do not need to rehearse in here. This is a hospital, when all's said and done–a place for rest and recuperation. You might be forgiven for being a little troubled, though–the Comte was a generous protector, was he not?"

"Generous and undemanding," Lillette answered. "No trophy of war could have wished for a better display-cabinet or to be polished in more delicate fashion. Forgive my sarcasm."

"There's nothing to forgive, child. You need not–must not–feel ashamed of your inability to feel the full force of your bereavement. I understand, perhaps better than you can imagine."

"Thank you, *Maître*," she said. "May I be impertinent, and question you about some related matters that *are* troubling me slightly?"

"Of course–but you must remember that I'm not a priest, and am not fit to hear confessions."

"I've seen you play a priest more than once," she told him, "not including false priests and spoiled priests, and I can honestly say that you put on a more convincing performance than any real priest I ever encountered. You've absolved my sins more generously and more comprehensively than any churchman ever could or would."

"You're very kind, my dear."

"Did you know my mother, Monsieur Moineaux?" the ex-*ingénue* asked, abruptly.

"Slightly," he replied. "We moved in the same social circles, but were placed at different points on their periphery. We must have been in the same room on may occasions, not infrequently involved in the same conversations, but we never spoke to one another *tête-à-tête*."

"And my father?"

"He deigned to look down his nose at me on several occasions. We might have spoken directly to one another once or twice, but I have to admit that I only knew him by reputation."

"My sisters?"

Moineaux did not know whether to smile or frown at her persistence. "Yes," he said, "I had the privilege of working with both of them, though only once with Juliette, before she became famous. I played several heroic roles opposite Ernestine."

"Was it Ernestine who asked you to look after me?"

"No one ever asked me to do that. You weren't yet born when I worked with Ernestine. Your father, mother and half-sisters were all dead before I was fully conscious of your existence."

"But you felt some lingering sense of obligation to one of them, at least?"

"Not at all. My brief relationship with Ernestine was exactly equivalent to Paul Damas' relationship with you, and of shorter duration. I thought her very beautiful, and delightful company, but it would have been reckless in the extreme to fall in love with her, even though her protector was not a military man. There was nothing romantic in our association."

"Thank you for not pretending that you don't know why I'm asking you these questions, Monsieur Moineaux," Lillette said, calmly. "You must know as well as I do what everyone assumes about the currency in which I paid you the price of my admission to your company. I've always denied it, but the fact that convention demands such denials has prevented anyone from taking the denial seriously. I'd always suspected, as my questions will have informed you, that you must have refrained from making such a demand because of some promise you had made in the distant past."

"Had we been living in a melodrama at the time I took you on, my dear, that would undoubtedly be the case," Moineaux said, lightly. "In reality, occurrences sometimes have simpler explanations, less tightly bound into the fabric of a plot. I'm not a young man, Lillette, and even in my younger days, I wasn't blessed–or cursed–with the hearty appetites of an authentic Don Juan. I've always found it ridiculously easy to avoid abusing my various privileges in that way. I claim no moral credit for it, mind, for I've certainly been prepared to profit from the desires of other men in exploiting your membership of my company, whether they were ordinary members of the Tragicomique's audience or enthusiasts of the late Comte's stripe. Don't paint me as any kind of saint, Lillette; I've been ruthless in my fashion, and you've little to thank me for."

"I know what I have to thank you for, Monsieur Moineaux," she said. "You didn't gift me with the Devil's beauty, but you've assisted me to use it far more profitably than I could ever have managed unaided."

"There's nothing diabolical about your beauty, my love. That's God's gift."

"But *the Devil's beauty* is what people call it, isn't it? Beauty is temptation made flesh; it persuades even the most skeptical of men to set reason aside and act on the basis of appetite."

"Doctor Louvois only thinks that he is the most skeptical of men," Moineaux observed. "He's a physician, after all–and all he did was let you in to see me, even though he had forbidden me visitors and I had consented to have them forbidden."

"I wasn't thinking of Doctor Louvois."

"No? You must be thinking of Simon's infatuation, then. But he's even less well-qualified as a skeptic and man of reason. He was arrogant enough to take the side of a humanized Mephistopheles in writing his play, but he mistakes the import of his own rhetoric. I can't imagine that he was convincing on stage as a demonized Faust, even with the aid of his remark-able new lenses, although I dare say that he relished the scenes he played with you in your courtesan role."

"He did," Lillette agreed. "He wasn't as good in the part as Paul, who is a far better actor, but there was a strange fervor in him. If you could have seen his eyes..."

"I did—and for what it may be worth, the strange fervor was probably produced by the laudanum he took to dull the sensitivity of his hearing. He saw something that troubled him in the Comte's eyes, although that was certainly not produced by any trick of optical artifice. Did you see that, perchance?"

"The Comte's eyes seemed very strange before the thrust that ended the duel," Lillette confirmed. "At the time, I couldn't imagine why he was alarmed—but if he felt a pain in his heart, because it was about to stop, that might explain it."

"It might indeed," Moineaux agreed. "Doctor Louvois advanced the same hypothesis, although Simon seemed less certain."

"Simon wasn't looking at the Comte dispassionately," Lillette observed. "He seems to have become infatuated with me, and is not actor enough to hide it. Because of his infatuation, he conceived a strong dislike for the Comte. Might that have affected the way he fought the duel, do you think? Might that be the reason he forgot his part, and thrust again when he should have been busy pretending to die?"

"It might," Moineaux conceded.

"No such emotion could have disturbed Paul's planning, of course," the ex-*ingénue* went on, "but the newspapers and the rumor-mongers seem particularly entranced by the mystery of the Comte's death. A whisper is flying around which says that Simon tricked the Comte into taking your part last night specifically in order to fight him, under conditions that gave him some kind of crucial supernatural advantage. I have heard it muttered, behind cupped hands, that Simon really is pos-sessed by the Devil—and that I, by implication, am the Devil's minion. It's silly gossip, of course, and I suppose it will do my shadowy reputation no harm... but something strange *is* happening, Monsieur Moineaux, even if it is not that. I don't know what it is, but I almost wish that I were capable of being frightened by it. As things are, all I seem to be able to feel is a vast indifference. I'm as utterly unmoved by Simon's love as I am by the Comte de Farineux's death–and that, surely, cannot be Godly?"

"Considering the present state of Creation," Moineaux murmured, "I'd be tempted to judge that there's nothing any-where near as Godly as vast indifference–but I don't mean to be flippant, my dear. I wonder if the triple shock of my close brush with death and the actual deaths of Hubert and the Comte might have left you uncharacteristically numb. Then again, the fact that Simon de Keramour appears to have fallen in love with you doesn't impose any similar obligation on you. He tries to cut a romantic figure, and represent himself as a man of mystery, but he only succeeds in seeming slightly silly. Although his oversensitive sight and hearing seem to be genuine afflictions rather than mere affectations, they are a handicap rather than an asset to his romantic pretensions."

"I'm not so shallow as to refuse to like a man because his eyes and ears are weak," Lillette told him, without any hint of reprimand. "There's something else about him that leaves me cold."

"He clings to the faults in his play as a miser to coin," Moineaux reflected. "That offends me far more than it offends you, of course, but it's symptomatic of a deeper malaise. He's an imperfect human being–but that's all that he is. He's not the Devil in disguise. If he were, he couldn't have lost control of himself to the point of violating his own scripted ending. Whatever possessed him last night, he was its victim, not its author."

"Faust, not Mephistopheles."

"Neither, my dear. *Le Nouveau Faust* is most certainly a human production, from its beginning to its unplayed end–and if there were a Devil, he certainly wouldn't waste his time interfering with a play staged at the Théâtre Tragicomique. If we're dealing with a supernatural agency here, it's a petty one that has not much room for maneuver. If God has given it permission to operate, He has not been excessively generous in the terms of His license. Personally, I'd rather see the affair in a different light, as a mischievous interference with the workings of chance by some impersonal *clinamen*."

"I've never heard the word, and have no idea what it means," Lillette confessed, blushing slightly.

"It comes from Lucretius' *De Rerum Natura*," Moineaux explained, "where the origin of all motion is credited to a tiny random swerve in the motion of a single atom falling through the void, which began a series of collisions that grew increasingly complex as time went by. Monsieur Jarry tried to reintroduce it into the parlance of the theater, to refer to an arbitrary shift in the unfolding pattern of a plot."

"I see. But our plot is moving in accordance with a highly ordered pattern, isn't it? The persistent shift is anything *but* random."

"True," Moineaux conceded. "Have you another term that we might use instead–once we have ruled out the Devil, of course?"

"No," she admitted, immediately moving on to say: "I wish you wouldn't get up today, Monsieur Moineaux. I don't want anything to happen to you, and I'm afraid that it will. I know that Simon is only rehearsing Monsieur Léchelier in case you can't get to the theater, but I wish you'd stay where you are, at least for one more day."

"Léchelier?" Moineaux echoed, incredulously. "Of all the men who might have volunteered... oh, I see. He was volunteered, in spite of himself, by Madame de Vernier. She'd far rather take up the sword herself, I dare say, but convention... well, I have no particular wish to do either of those two specimens a service, but I can't stand back and let a man risk his life, even if it is Léchelier. Nor can I stand back and let an imbecile like him take to the boards of *my* theater in the ranks of *my* company. Tonight, Lillette, I'll play my part or die trying–and I won't be in the least offended if you can't find anything in your heart to mark my passing but vast indifference."

"No, Monsieur," the actress murmured. "For you, I'll mourn."

"Except that no one is going to die," Moineaux said, quick to recover the situation. "I'm better now, no matter what Louvois may think–and I have a plan. Tonight, my love, we shall play our parts with a brilliance that has not been seen before at the Tragicomique. We'll put an end to this deadly pattern. It won't matter what we choose to call it, because we'll never have to refer to it again, except in memory–and it will fade from memory very quickly, I suspect, to become a ghostly legend, repeated in disbelief for mere amusement's sake."

"Even so..." Lillette began–but she did not seem displeased to be interrupted.

"You'll be brilliant, my dear," Moineaux told her. "Tonight, we shall make history–and the one thing that will not be forgotten will be the magnificence of your beauty and our performance. That should not be insulted by the presence of a half-man like Léchelier. I shall be there, my darling, because that is fate's desire, and fate's requirement. Whatever the outcome, I shall be there. I would not dare to make the promise to anyone else, and I must ask you not to repeat it, but I make the promise to you as solemnly as a wedding vow. I shall be there, to make your fortune secure."

She frowned as well as blushing, and Moineaux knew that she really had taken slight offense at the implication that she might be thinking of her own benefit instead of his, but she nodded her lovely head with all her natural grace. He was confident, of course, that the inevitable result of his instruction would be that everyone in Paris, with the possible exception of Emile Louvois, would know by 7:30 that Stéphane Moineaux would be appearing on stage at the Tragicomique that evening, defying the Devil to do his worst.

20

Obtaining his release from the hospital was not as difficult as Moineaux had feared; he was not, in the end, compelled to make his escape as if from prison. Once Emile Louvois was convinced that Moineaux could not be dissuaded from rising from his sick-bed–while being fully aware neither the hospital's surgeons nor the Sisters of Mercy were inclined to wrestle rebellious patients into submission and frog-march them back to bed– he contented himself with issuing dire warnings and washing his hands of all responsibility. He strongly advised the actor-manager to have stretcher-bearers waiting in the wings in case he collapsed on stage, were he to get that far.

"After the last three performances," Moineaux assured him, "there will most certainly be stretcher-bearers waiting in the wings, and a fast carriage just outside the stage door. You might well see me again, in a mere matter of hours."

"It's more than probable, in my judgement," the physician replied. "I only hope that you will still be able to see and hear me, so that I can remind you that I told you so."

Simon de Keramour had sent his *coupé* to collect his co-star, and Marianne Jonquille was waiting with it to help him up into the interior.

"This is madness," she told him, only a little drunkenly, as the carriage moved off. "Sheer pig-headed madness."

"I quite agree," Moineaux told her. "Exhilarating, isn't it?"

"The laudanum's gone to your head," she told him. "You're not used to it. The doctor obviously overestimated the dose."

"I refused medication last night," Moineaux replied, "so the magnitude of the dose he might have offered is quite irrelevant. I have taken none today, and will go on stage in a far calmer state of mind than Simon de Keramour."

"Or me–that's what you're implying, isn't it?"

"I wouldn't dream of it, my dear."

"Don't be cruel, Stéphane," she instructed him, need-lessly. "If the graze in your heart opens up and begins shedding blood too liberally, or the strain allows a presently-latent infection to begin a rapid increase and start a fever, you might find yourself in a situation in which you'd be better off minimizing the debts you'll have to pay in Purgatory."

"I feel quite well," Moineaux assured her.

This was a lie. The actor had contrived to dress himself without increasing the pain in his chest too dramatically, but walking down the steps of the hospital's meager perron had proved unexpectedly taxing. The pain in his breast was still dull as he settled into the cushions of the carriage, but the manner in which it increased with every movement–especially movements involving any kind of stretching–suggested that the final dueling scene might be a drastic trial by ordeal, no matter which of the combatants were eventually to claim the apparent victory. Mercifully, there were no rough roads between the hospital and the theater, and the upward slopes were relatively gentle. Moineaux was able to sit quite still without being bounced about overmuch.

At the theater, everyone was waiting to greet him and cheer his brave return–including a considerable crowd that had gathered in the street outside, which had to be restrained by a company of gendarmes. Although he was saved from any serious jostling, his head began to ache as he hurried through the stage door and made for his private dressing-room.

Once Moineaux was safely ensconced in his sanctuary, however, Paul Damas insistently claimed the privilege of being alone with him, Moineaux tried to refuse, but his protests were overridden.

"You must not do this, *Maître*," the *jeune premier* said. "It's too dangerous. Let me go on in your place. If they arrest me afterwards, I shall claim that my understanding was that I was only banned from playing my own part, and that allowing you to play yours would have been tantamount to culpable homicide. I know the moves perfectly, *Maître*, and I know that

I can win the fight, even if the Devil himself takes possession of Monsieur de Keramour's arm."

"That isn't what's happening, my friend," Moineaux told him. "Please heed my good advice–and trust me. I have a plan. Leave me alone now, and let me get ready."

"There are a thousand rumors abroad," Paul said, making no move to leave "and no one, including you, can possibly know what to believe–but Simon de Keramour told me what you said to him at the hospital last night. The brute facts are the same, no matter what we call the threat that is hanging over us. The pattern has to be broken. The Comte could not do it, but *I can*. If Mephistopheles has to win the final battle in order to put a stop to the sequence of catastrophes, I am the man to do it. Let me try, I beg you."

"No, Paul, you're not the man to do it," Moineaux told him, wearily. "No one will take my place tonight unless I drop dead before the play begins–and if I do, it will be Léchelier who takes my place."

"He's not even a fencing-master, let alone an actor!" Paul complained. "You can't possibly allow de Keramour to put him on."

"Oh, I won't have to," Moineaux said, impatiently. "If the question were even to arise, I'd be dead–and as you see, I'm very much alive."

"How will you defend yourself, Monsieur?" the younger actor demanded, rudely. "You're not much of a swordsman without the benefit of a script, and you've dragged yourself from a hospital bed against your physician's advice. How will you parry that awful riposte?"

"I've survived the thrust once," Moineaux told him, making every possible effort to regain complete command of his own composure, although his headache was getting worse with every sentence that spilled from Paul's lips. "In any case, I intend to subvert it before it happens. I believe that I can do that. Please go away–I need to be by myself."

"I won't go," Paul said, flatly. "Marianne is right. You've overdosed on laudanum and lost yourself in a delusion. I won't let you go on."

Moineaux would gladly have strangled the young man at that moment, but he could see that a different approach was required. He had to appear calm, and master of his situation.

"Don't be ridiculous, Paul," he said, trying not to sound hostile. "I know what I'm doing. I insisted from the very beginning that the play needed rewriting. Its author disagreed—but it's by no means impossible, or even unusual, for an author to be blind to some of the questions implicit in his own work. It's often the case that it isn't until a play is brought to life in a theater, by a careful director, that its fundamental impetus becomes obvious. That's why it has to be me, Paul, not you or anyone else, who takes the stage tonight. I'm no swordsman, it's true. I'm not a playwright either, for all my genius in adaptation—but I *am* an actor, and a great one, no matter how lackluster my performances has been of late. I couldn't have written a new *Faust*, but I understand the one than Monsieur de Keramour has written better than he does. I understand my own part *much* better than he does. I know how the play ought to end. I was confused, at first, but I'm not confused any longer. I needed that tiny scratch on my heart and three days of bed-rest to clarify my intellect—but it's clear enough now. I believe I know how to end the play. Perhaps I'm wrong—but I need to try. No one else can do it. Now, I'm no longer begging you but ordering you to go outside and stand guard on my door. Let no one else in. I need you to do that, Paul—you have to help me."

The strategy worked. Given an explicit duty to fulfill, Paul was spared the necessity of inventing one. He got up at last, and took up his sentry-duty as ordered. Moineaux heard him turn away three other contenders avid to serve as Job's comforters, evidently rejoicing in his license to be insistent.

When the actor-manager was finally ready to face his company again, with his make-up and his initial costume in place and his headache soothed by stillness, he stepped out of the tiny room. He did not give Paul an opportunity to speak before issuing him with new orders and new responsibilities.

"I may need some assistance with my costume-changes," he said, "so you must make certain that everything's in place and ready–especially the blood-bag that accompanies my final outfit."

"Blood-bag?" Paul echoed. "But you're not using the blood-bags, or the pointed blades. You'll surely be doing it the old-fashioned way, just as the company did last night."

"That didn't save the Comte's life," Moineaux pointed out. "Monsieur de Keramour and I intend to do the scene as it was originally planned, with pointed blades and blood-bags. The old-fashioned ways are obsolete–we're only 18 months away from a new century. The play's the important thing, my dear boy–if the play is right, everything will go to plan. Hush now–the curtain's about to go up and it's time for my entrance!"

The *jeune premier* shook his head, sadly. "You should have let me take your place, *Maître*," he said, automatically dropping his voice to a whisper at the mention of the curtain going up. "You really should."

"One day, you will," Moineaux promised him. "Not tonight, though." He walked to the wings as steadily as he could, trying with all his might to give the appearance of a man without a care in the world. Paul walked beside him, ready to lend a supportive arm, but it proved unnecessary, even though they were briefly interrupted by an encounter with Monsieur Léchelier, whose backstage presence was strongly reminiscent of a fish out of water. He had the good sense not to block Moineaux's path, but he insisted on favoring the actor-manager with a stiff bow and an uncommonly warm expression of heartfelt gratitude.

"My condolences to Madame de Vernier," Moineaux murmured. "I dedicate tonight's performance to the late Comte, who will be missed at the Tragicomique as in the whole of Paris."

"Thank you, Monsieur," Léchelier replied. "Thank you."

In spite of this delay, Moineaux and Paul arrived at the appropriate station in the wings with a full three minutes still in hand before the curtain went up.

To avoid further questions, Moineaux seized the opportunity to move the end of the curtain aside and peep through the gap into the crowded auditorium. It was extremely satisfactory to see such a full house for once, and so many well-dressed patrons—but what gave Moineaux far more satisfaction than the prospect of so many fashionably-dressed men and their gorgeously-clad companions drawn up in neat and near-uniform ranks was the sight of an entire row of the stalls whose members were costumed much more variously.

Alfred Villette was formally dressed, of course, but his wife Marguerite—better known as Rachilde—had put on one of her most flamboyant evening-dresses. Jean Lorrain was playing the dandy wholeheartedly, in his ever-extravagant fashion. Although Jarry had forsworn his bicycle shorts for grey flannel trousers, he was wearing a purple jacket and a huge lemon yellow cravat. Apollinaire had evidently attempted to match him, although his coat was more puce than purple and his cravat was orange. Marcel Schwob wore a conventional black jacket, but even he had put on a salmon-pink waistcoat, presumably in honor of the sacred memory of Théophile Gautier's *grand geste* at the first performance of Victor Hugo's *Hernani*. Catulle Mendès had done the same, and seemed a trifle disgruntled by the discovery that he had been anticipated. Albert Robida had also elected to dress in satirical fashion, but as he was seated between Mendès and Octave Uzanne, only two places away from Raymond Roussel, he did not stand out at all. Colette, in amazon guise, and her husband Willy were dressed in carefully matched costumes, which gained in flair by being bracketed by two individuals in monks' robes, both of whom had their hoods pulled up to conceal their faces. The Rosny brothers formed another matching pair, but they formed a group in relatively orthodox costume with Paul Bourget and Henri Régnier.

"My God!" said Paul Damas, who had craned his neck in order to see what Moineaux was looking at with such evident fascination. "Isn't that Anatole France? There's Pierre Loti! And Jules Verne! And that's surely Emile Zola on the end of the row! But who on Earth are the monks?"

"One is certainly Huysmans," Moineaux told him. "The other, I strongly suspect, is Rémy de Gourmont–it must be the first time he's ventured out of his apartment this year. Do you see who's sitting next to him, though? That's Oscar Wilde! He's rumored to be as gravely ill as I am. It would be only slightly less astonishing to see Rimbaud and Verlaine. Jarry didn't know until this morning that I intended to appear tonight, and he could hardly be entirely confident that I would, but see what he has accomplished! Given that he only bought 21 tickets, two of the others must have paid for their own!"

"But why?" Paul asked. "Why would Monsieur Jarry take so much trouble, even if you did do him the favor of producing one of his plays when no one else would?"

"That's not the reason," Moineaux replied. "I suspect that you might have more to do with his reckless purchase than I do. He heard your speech, on the night you killed me–and understood the import of what had happened. He guessed what I'd have to do tonight–and if he's guessed right, then so have I. And now, dear boy–I'm on!"

21

The first act of *Le Nouveau Faust* was performed exactly as Simon de Keramour had written it, at least insofar as the words were concerned. Moineaux played the opening scene with his servant easily enough, although he remained seated throughout. His headache remained a sullen presence at the back of his mind, but there were no alarm signals from his pleural cavity.

When Simon de Keramour made his first entrance as Mephistopheles, Jean Faust was supposed to become more active, in order to increase the theatricality of the confrontation, but Moineaux kept to his seat. The playwright's black contact lenses fitted in very well with his costume–which was far less extraordinary than traditional caricaturish representations equipped with horns and a tail–adding a useful subtle implication of diabolism. If the Breton had dosed himself with laudanum again to protect his sensitive hearing generating a headache of his own, the drug's effects were not yet obvious.

The scene went well enough–as was only to be expected, since little enough was expected of it. Moineaux recited his allotted lines with no other purpose in mind but to get through the preliminaries. The first phase of any literary endeavor, he knew, had to be regarded as a foundation; it was only in the later phases that a play could develop a natural momentum of its own, demanding a particular sequence of extrapolations and–eventually–aesthetically-satisfactory closure. Act One of *Le Nouveau Faust*, like Act One of any other three-act play, defined the project and set its parameters, putting the precedents in place that would demand and compel elaboration and development.

Moineaux's fellow players delivered performances that were perfectly satisfactory, despite Moineaux's own carefully-restricted movements and Simon de Keramour's obvious lack of experience as a *jeune premier*. Lillette was exceptionally good, in spite of her recent tragedy, although she had little more to do than establish her character, and Marianne was perfectly adequate in registering her presence and defining her character's relationship with Lillette's. The final scene of the act, in which Moineaux-as-Faust and Simon-as-Mephistopheles concluded their bargain and completed their exchange of appearances, provided an adequate sub-climax, and the fact that Jean Faust was able to become vigorously active in his new body while Mephistopheles was compelled to slump into virtual lassitude presumably helped to communicate the full significance of the exchange to the duller members of the audience.

Moineaux came off-stage without experiencing any undue discomfort and shrugged off the whispered concerns of his fellow players, but his hand was shaking as he accepted a glass of water and sipped from it with careful restraint.

Act Two started quietly enough, but soon accelerated as Simon-as-Faust was moved by the energy of his unorthodox rejuvenation to make the acquaintance of Lillette in her second guise. Moineaux was able to watch the first phase of their interaction from the wings, and grudgingly conceded that the playwright's attraction to Lillette worked to the advantage of her portrayal of a personification of lust.

The momentum of the play slowed considerably as it ventured in the direction of greater profundity, in the scene in which Lillette–having changed her costume and resumed the role of Marguerite–consulted her tutor regarding the impact of Lamarckian evolutionary theory on the idea of progress, and the import of the combination in respect of the human condition and its attendant ambitions. Moineaux established himself in an armchair again, but dared not relax into its cushions because he knew that he had to concentrate much harder now.

"If every organism that exists," the pupil said, entirely obedient to authorial instruction, "from the humblest diatom or worm to human beings, is possessed by an innate impetus to improvement, and the capacity to improve by means of relentless effort, then how can we regard our species, or ourselves, as finished?"

"We cannot," her tutor answered, supposedly speaking now as a demon rather than as a man. "No work of creation is ever finished, whether it be a man, a spirit, a play, an Earth, a Paradise or an Inferno. The ferment goes ever on. Religion tells us that immortality brings completion, but it only brings suspension, and suspension can no more endure forever than chaos. Immortality is an illusion, destined to fail–and an immortal who learns that lesson might reckon himself fortunate, for all that it informs him of the one unacceptable fact of life."

"What fact is that?" Lillette asked, picking up the cue with fluid ease, even though it was formulated slightly differently in the script.

"Foreknowledge of death," Moineaux-as-Mephistopheles replied. "Humans, I know, consider that a dire curse, although it is the inevitable corollary of rational calculation. In order to anticipate the transactions of the elements and the mechanism of the world, and thus acquire the gift of choice, it is necessary to know that one must eventually die."

"And yet," Lillette observed, seizing the opportunity to return to the words written in the script, "the impetus to progress remains, futile though it seems. Are organisms foolish, then, to strive as Monsieur Lamarck observes? Or should we be content to know that what we achieve will benefit our descendants, endowing our children with better gifts than those we inherited in embryo?"

At this point in Simon de Keramour's extrapolation of the situation he had derived, Mephistopheles was supposed to communicate to the audience the effect that Marguerite's presence was having on his humanized intellect and romantic inclinations. He was supposed to be moved to a kind of ecstasy—but Moineaux's response to the momentum of the play was different in kind and quality. The subsequent course of the discussion was supposed to include an account of Mephistopheles' vision of the scientific cosmos, informed by that same ecstasy. It was also to include a discourse on the importance of choice in selecting a direction of progress, in both the political context—as exemplified by Napoleon and his imperial ambitions—and the personal one, as exemplified by Marguerite's ambition to make progress in social and intellectual *milieux* dominated by the male of the species.

Moineaux-as-Mephistopheles, however, exercised his own power of choice in selecting a subtly different tack. "The impetus to progress is not what Lamarck imagined," he stated. "Nor are the rewards of endeavor as he conceived them. Yes, it befits us to leave legacies behind, so that our children and our civilization will have greater wealth at their disposal than we had. We should, at least, make certain that we do not leave the world poorer than we found it–that is elementary generosity, the oxygen of good–but we are not here on Earth to serve the ends of evolution or progress, any more than the merest diatom or worm. In that respect, the bacilli that spoil and consume our flesh, enfevering the living and rotting the dead, make a better contribution to the scheme of things than we do, for they are the principal agents of natural selection, which eliminate the feeble and provide a challenge to the strong. Were human beings merely to use the power of choice to serve the ends of evolution, we would do that most efficiently by becoming ever-more-efficient killing machines, destroying other species and refining our own by rigorous and promiscuous murder."

Lillette showed her true colors then, for the words she had memorized and rehearsed gave her no help at all in formulating a reply to that unexpected observation. "Is that not the way the world is going, *Maître*?" she said. "What do you imagine this 19th century will be like, if not a riot of ingenious and bloody warfare, and a martyrization of Nature?"

"Perhaps it will, if the demons inherent in our flesh have their way," the disguised Mephistopheles replied, "but we need not sell ourselves to those demons, if we can discover pride enough to refuse. Even if the bargain is made, and the carnival of destruction born of the Terror continues to gather force until it becomes a costumed hurricane, we shall not be damned, provided that we can see through the sham to the reality beneath, and understand what we really are and ought to be."

"And what are we, really, *Maître*?" Lillette asked, perhaps speaking as much for herself as for Jean Faust's Marguerite. "What ought we to try to be?"

"We are actors, my love," the false Faust declared. "Which is to say that, unlike bacilli or diatoms, worms or cockroaches, rats or birds of paradise, we are capable of deciding what and who we shall pretend to do and be."

"We have the faculty of choice," Marguerite said, recognizing a move in the direction of the script. "Even women have the power of free will, although we have rarely been enthusiastic to exercise it."

"That faculty, and something more important," Moineaux said, ignoring the cue and its invitation to return to Simon de Keramour's concerns. "We have the faculty of concealing, complicating and confusing our choices. We have the power of pretense, of ambiguity, of art. We can do, and be, more than one thing at the same time. We are not imprisoned by customs, habits, rules and patterns, We can tell lies and offer rival interpretations. That, my dear, is the essence of humankind and human mind."

Lillette had been standing all this time, but now she moved to the arm of Moineaux's chair and perched upon it, careful not to obscure him from the audience. "Go on, *Maître*," she invited, when he paused for breath.

"We do not have to follow our scripts, no matter how well-wrought they are," Moineaux went on, "nor how deeply ingrained they seem to be in our motor reflexes. We are not merely secondary creators but creators in every sense of the word. There is infinitely more that a man might do with a soul than defend its purity or sell it. And that, my dear, is why I am no longer the Jean Faust you knew yesterday, nor the Mephistopheles that the Devil's script desires to make of me."

Lillette leapt up then, and feigned alarm. "What is Mephistopheles?" she said "How are you other than Jean Faust?"

"In the same sense that you are other than the Marguerite you were a day ago," Moineaux told her. "We all renew ourselves, hour by hour, and are sometimes surprised by what we become–but we should not be surprised, my dear, even if our limbs sometimes seem obedient to another will than our own. We may take alarm, if we find ourselves inclined to strange new passions or strange new frailties, but we should not be surprised–and we should not count ourselves helpless, either."

"It is easy for a man to say that," Lillette replied, finding yet another opportunity to deliver another of Simon de Keramour's lines, "but far less easy for a woman."

"It's not so easy, even for a man," he told her, "but those of us fortunate enough to be born human, and those beneficiaries of progressive evolution who increase their humanity, must learn to manage their renewal, lest they lose the prerogatives of choice to the exercise of mere appetites."

"When I say that it is less easy for a woman to say that than a man, *Maître*," the pupil protested, "I mean that a woman begins from a position in which the range of her choices is far more limited. No matter how strong her innate impulse to progress might be, she is faced with obstacles that limit her in the direction as well as the velocity of her progress."

"True," Moineaux's character conceded. "But some, at least, of those obstacles are delusional—and others can be overcome. The same is true, I think, of my own predicament—and that is the key to the enigma, the solution to the puzzle. I think I see the logic of the situation now, and the nature of the trap into which my counterpart and I have fallen. I shall not be fooled again by shallow trickery and a seductive script. I am beginning to know who and what I really am—and my advice to you, as a good tutor speaking to his faithful pupil, is to discover who and what you are, not by seeking mental solace and social advancement in philosophical learning, or comfort and luxury in the traffic of lust, but in becoming a true and honest actor."

"I needed no tutor to tell me *that*, *Maître* Faust," Lillette answered, in a voice hardly above a whisper—which could nevertheless be clearly heard in the upper circle. "But it's not advice that's easy to follow is it—no matter who we think we are, or who we really are? You ought to remember, Monsieur Faust, the impetus to progress possessed by humble folk like you and me often lacks passion as well as strength."

None of that was in the script, and the deviation was entirely unnecessary; Lillette could easily have stuck to her lines, without the slightest threat to the continuity of the scene. Moineaux smiled, in frank delight.

"I know that only too well," Moineaux's character declared, "and always did know it, although I've often been unable to admit it. You're right to remind me that I'm as humble in my actual status as you or anyone–but I *can* play my part. You shall see that I can play my part, though all the devils in Hell might try to seize my arm or strike me down!"

And with that, the once-great actor came forcefully to his feet and made his exit, as carefully as he could on slightly unsteady feet. He was suddenly painfully conscious of the fact that the wound in his breast had opened slightly, and was leaking blood into the bandage wrapped around is torso. As soon as he as off stage, he paused, groping for support–but Paul was in the wings on the other side of the stage, and it was Simon de Keramour who put an arm around him to sustain him.

"That was a travesty," the playwright hissed into his ear. "There was no need to alter my lines, and it was certainly no improvement. Delirium is taking hold of you, and the only way to resist it is to *say the lines as I have written them.*"

There was no time for Moineaux to reply, even if he had wanted to. The playwright had to go on again, as the rejuvenated and invulnerable Faust, to make his second rendezvous with Lillette Fevret and imperious lust, and to fight his first duel.

Deprived of the supporting arm, Moineaux seized the curtain in his right hand, and gripped it very firmly. He drew deep breaths in a carefully measured fashion, and tried to will the pain in his chest into submission. He succeeded, but the only result was to make his headache seem worse by comparison. It had taken on a feverish quality–but he could not tell, as yet, whether that was the result of excitement, inspiration, or an infection that would make him mad before destroying him.

"I have a choice," he murmured, in a voice inaudible to anyone but himself. "I have only to make it correctly, and death shall not have me. I have only to find the right pattern, and the wrong one will be shattered forever. I can do it–and there are 23 authors sitting in the stalls who will think far less of me than I deserve if I do not do it *well*."

Paul arrived then, having made his way around from the other side of the stage, to help sustain him until Simon de Keramour and Fernand Cornu had concluded the first of the play's two armed conflicts. Moineaux watched as Fernand fell down and played dead, without sustaining a scratch or missing a heartbeat. Fernand, at least, had played his part effortlessly in every performance so far.

Simon de Keramour concluded the scene with a flourish, and the curtain fell on Act Two. Paul Damas helped Moineaux back to his dressing-room, so that he could change for his final confrontation.

22

While Lillette-as-Lust-Personified, Marianne and Simon de Keramour played out their scenes in the first part of Act Three, Moineaux was able to take as much time as he needed to adjust the dressing on his actual wound and accommodate the bladder full of fake blood snugly within his costume. Paul Damas watched him, shaking his head sadly, for all the world as if he were a worldly wise old man and Moineaux a mere intemperate youth.

"I don't understand what you were trying to do out there in Act Two," Paul told him. "I confess that I couldn't tell, at times, whether you were speaking as Jean Faust, the demon Mephistopheles or Stéphane Moineaux."

"In the theater," Moineaux told him, placidly, "everything is ambiguous and ambiguity is everything."

"You've always been able to reel off high-sounding lines by the score, Monsieur Moineaux," Paul said, "but I've never been entirely convinced that you knew or cared what they were supposed to mean. You and I are melodramatists by vocation, of course, always more interested in momentary effects than enduring wisdom, but your present plight is serious and you might do better to take a calmer and more considered view of your final speech, if you get that far without disaster striking. There are great men in your audience."

"But not on my stage, eh, Paul? You find my philosophy unconvincing—just so much theatrical hot air?"

"I fear for you, *Maître*. Doctor Louvois warned Marianne on Sunday that if your wound were infected, the infection might not begin to show its effects until today. He has been satisfied with your progress, I know—but that possibility still exists. If you exert yourself as the dueling scene requires, the germs might multiply at a terrific rate. You seem feverish now, *Maître*, and I cannot help wondering whether your eloquence might be edging towards delirious incoherence."

"Very delicately put," Moineaux said, with only a hint of a sneer. "There's certainly a possibility that I'm mad, or worse, but that doesn't relieve me of the responsibility of acting as I see fit."

"Let me go on in your stead," Paul demanded, again.

"No. I must carry the plan through; to do otherwise would be to admit defeat. Even if this were Hell, and the play my punishment, I would still have to *play my part*."

"This is certainly not Hell, *Maître*," Paul assured him. "It's Paris. I can't believe that there's a Tragicomique in Hell, but if there is, it would surely be forbidden to you, like the rations of Tantalus. Is there *any* melodrama in Hell, do you suppose? Or is there nothing else?"

"That's better," Moineaux said. "A little wit, delivered light-heartedly. Is that a cool breeze I feel? Of course there's melodrama in Hell, and it is all tragicomic in its composition. Purgatory might be a different proposition, though—and Limbo too."

"And what of Paradise?"

169

"Oh, there's no melodrama in Heaven," Moineaux said, scornfully. "That's why no one ever goes there."

"Do you ever really know or care what you're saying, *Maître*?" Paul asked, more earnestly than the build-up to the question seemed to warrant, "or is it all pure performance: an irrepressible haemorrhage of spontaneous *ad libs*?"

"That's very good, Paul," Moineaux said. "I shall steal that some day, if I survive Act Three. Am I really giving the impression of being victim to wayward delirium?"

"Yes, *Maître*. You *are* feverish. Your face is very florid, despite your make-up, and I can literally feel the heat radiating from your body. Such an appearance might not be unbecoming to a demon in human guise, of course... but it's not feigned, and I truly fear for your life and your sanity. You're beginning to tremble, I believe. If some wicked spirit employing Simon de Keramour's physique wants to run you through, I can't believe that you'll be able to parry the thrust."

"What worries me more," Moineaux told him, in a tone now quite devoid of sarcasm, "is whether he'll be able to parry mine, if something wicked takes possession of *me*." He had to go then, in order to take up his position in the wings, ready for his final entrance.

Marianne left the stage a minute or so before Moineaux went on. As she passed him by she looked him up and down, with anxiety written clearly in her features, but she was too much the professional to say anything to him, or even to pause in her flight, lest she distract him from his cue.

Simon and Lillette concluded their scripted dialogue, and Moineaux moved out into the field of the lights. The script specified that, in his capacity as the marginally-humanized Mephistopheles, he was supposed to inform Jean Faust that the time had come for the settlement of their bargain. Simon, in his capacity as the marginally-demonized Faust, was then supposed to complain that the agreed term had not yet elapsed. The actor-manager no longer had the slightest intention of following the script, however, save only for the moves of the fight itself.

"You must leave that demoiselle alone now, Mephistopheles," Moineaux said, soberly. "It is time for this sham to end and the truth to be recognized."

He saw a flash of surprise in Lillette's eyes, but it probably could not have compared with the invisible astonishment in Simon de Keramour's carefully-shielded eyes. The playwright had to make a sensible response—and thus far, in tonight's performance, he had not been required to divert from his own script by a single word. There was nothing in his script, though, that could possibly serve as a reply to what Moineaux had just said.

"Why do *you* call me Mephistopheles?" the author demanded, less coolly than he probably intended. "You know full well that I am Jean Faust—and that I have no further business with you for some time to come. Begone, and leave me to my pleasure."

"You are not Jean Faust and never have been," Moineaux said, calmly. "You have been deluded, as have I. We have both been tricked by a whim of circumstance, and the bargain we imagined having made is quite worthless."

"That is not true!" Simon de Keramour exclaimed, with an asperity the audience might have thought undue. "I know who and what I am, and if you think otherwise you are mad! I *know* what the truth of this situation is, and there is no one in this world or any other who has authority to deny it."

Simon de Keramour had left Lillette's side now, and had moved to confront Moineaux. The ex-*ingénue* had withdrawn to her appointed spot at the rear of the stage and to the left, leaving the principal space free for the conflict to come.

"You have mistaken yourself, Mephistopheles," Moineaux's character told Simon de Keramour's. "I understand why you have done so, but the time has come for the farce to end. You have imagined, for a while, that you were Jean Faust, gifted with a new and virile body, and that I was Mephistopheles, banished for a while into your own enfeebled frame by some diabolical metempsychosis—but the Devil is an idle spirit, and all he did was to cast shadows upon our minds.

171

You, as his minion, were completely deluded, and genuinely believed that you had been remade as Jean Faust–but I am a man of science, who knows how to ply Ockham's razor. It did not take me long to realize that I am still Jean Faust, who had merely been tricked for the briefest of intervals into believing that I was a demon in human form."

"Nonsense!" the desperate author protested. "Madness! You are trying to send me early to my damnation, because you cannot bear to wait–but it will not work. It *cannot* work. I *am* Faust, and I will not be damned. Do you hear me, demon, *I will not be made a liar, and I will not be damned!*"

"I hear you, Father of Lies," Moineaux's character said, his voice still silkily calm and his stance still motionless. "But no one will be damned tonight who is not already damned–and I dare to hope that even he might escape, if he has any but the slightest claim on the privilege of existence. I am Jean Faust, and I intend to reclaim the whole of my identity and freedom of action from the toils of delusion. If you hope to deny me that, then we must fight–but you cannot win, for I am fighting for the truth against a lie, and the truth must out in the end. That is what science says, and what science is."

"No!" Simon de Keramour's character retorted. "I am Faust, and cannot doubt it. I have my identity, and freedom from delusion. If you say otherwise, then we must certainly fight–but you are the one who cannot win. I am young and you are old. I am a creator, and you a mere actor. I have every strength and virility that a man can possess, and you can hardly stand unaided. If we fight, Mephistopheles, you will die, just as everyone else who has faced my blade has died."

"No, Mephistopheles," said Moineaux, allowing his voice to take on a hint of regret, mingling sadness with pity. "I shall not die as others have–for I have always known, without quite bringing the fact to the surface of consciousness until now, that I never was Mephistopheles. I have always known, moreover, that it was Mephistopheles I had to fight. Not merely on my own behalf but on behalf of all the men who have been in my place before and might have stood in my place in the future. No self-deluding demon can prevail against me, for I am what I am and who I am: an actor, in every sense of the word. *En garde*, false fiend! Let us see which of us the hand of fate will favor this time."

Moineaux saw Simon de Keramour's eyes flash, then, in spite of their Stygian blackness–not with a bright star of anger, but with a diffuse gleam of alarm.

The younger man struck first, just as the script demanded–and the moves unfolded in perfect accord with those the playwright had determined and rehearsed, step by step by step.

Moineaux took the first apparent wound, the fake blood soaking his sleeve and liberally splashing his torso. Simon took the second, and the third, his own shirt becoming drenched with vivid red.

They moved smoothly, like clockwork, but Moineaux knew what that apparent smoothness was costing him. He knew that there was real blood mingling with the false, and that his head was on fire. He knew that a single authentic thrust, properly intended to strike home, might be unstoppable–unless some mysterious supernatural agency came to his aid. Even so, he continued to play his part, ignoring the pain in his chest, the agony in his head and the weariness in his limbs.

He began a mental count-down to the scheduled climax of the duel, when the final flurry of blows was due to be exchanged.

When his silent count reached zero, Moineaux struck– and Simon de Keramour, as if in the grip of a compulsion far more powerful than his own dull will, parried the blow and made his astonishing riposte.

Moineaux could not block the thrust, neither could he stand aside–and yet, when the point of the author's sword surely should have bitten into his breast, slipped between his ribs and slit his heart in two, he was no longer there... or, if he *was* there, was also *not there*, despite that God and Nature alike ruled such a trick impossible.

At any rate, the riposte did him no harm–and when Moineaux's character thrust again, on his own account, Simon de Keramour's final blood-bag burst, for the first time in any performance of his play, and a huge gout of red arterial blood jetted forth, bringing a loud gasp of horror and surprise from the audience-who had not expected that at all.

Lillette screamed, and her scream woke echoes behind the scenery and in the swings, as well as the circle and the stalls.

Moineaux imagined that he saw the horror and the terror in his opponent's jet black eyes, and knew that Doctor Louvois had said no more than the simple truth when he had claimed that a man really might die of fright, if he believed in the imaginary thing that threatened him.

Simon de Keramour fell backwards, deprived of the power to stand upright or support himself in any fashion at all. The playwright's head hit the boards of the stage with a sickening thud that must have knocked him unconscious, if he were still alive.

The curtain came down then, lowered in panic in response to Lillette's scream, having been held at the ready by the anticipation of disaster–but Stéphane Moineaux stepped outside the line of its fall with a very easy stride, and turned to face the audience from the forestage.

"Ladies and gentlemen," he said. "As you have seen–and as you probably half-expected, there has been an unfortunate accident."

23

"I dare say that you are slightly confused," the lone fig-ure on the forestage went on, "as to whether I am speaking to you in the character of Jean Faust, or merely as Stéphane Moineaux, the director of Monsieur de Keramour's play and owner of the Théâtre Tragicomique, or perhaps as some strange amalgam of the two. To tell the truth, I am not entirely certain myself–but one thing I can say without fear of contra-diction is that I am not possessed by Mephistopheles. That possession was always an illusion, and it has now been ban-ished–exorcised, if that is the term some of you would prefer.

"I can say, too–again, without fear of contradiction–that the unscripted riposte which somehow intruded itself into the climactic duel in each of the play's performances to date will not be seen again. It too has been banished–the curse is bro-ken, if you will. You may wonder how I can know this to be true, but I assure you that it *is* true. As the winner of the duel that has just taken place–the unexpected winner, I suppose, although my victory was written in the script–my character is fully entitled to claim the privilege of stating the moral and meaning of the event, and as the victorious Jean Faust, I swear by Almighty God and Auguste Comte alike that from now on, the duel will be fought fairly, and its end will be safely con-fined by the limits of possibility.

"To those who have imagined that the theater or the play was cursed, I say that it is cursed no more–and to those of you who abhor the very thought of curses, and all such nonsense, I say that superstition has been defeated, and the rule of natural law restored.

"I am not myself–whether I speak as Jean Faust, or Sté-phane Moineaux, or both–a believer in curses, but I am a be-liever in evolution and progress. The Chevalier de Lamarck, who was a living and exciting presence in the world at the time Monsieur de Keramour's play is set, is no longer with us, but his spirit lives on in Henri Bergson, the celebrant of the world's perpetual state of becoming. With the aid of their philosophy, I can accept the hypothesis that individual organisms and the universe entire are in a state of permanent change, ever striving for innovation, never content with any apparent completion. If that is so, then it might not be the sole prerogative of the busy human mind to search so assiduously for patterns as to find them even when they have no basis in reality, but are merely haphazard combinations and strange echoes. Perhaps the universe itself, in the constant process of its own reproduction and reinvention, finds a certain fascination in the multiplication of strange echoes, and is forever experimenting with bizarre coincidence.

"Jean Faust, I think, would favor that explanation, if it can qualify as an explanation. As for Stéphane Moineaux... well, that is a more complicated issue.

"In speaking to you as Stéphane Moineaux, I have to admit that common sense points in the direction of a very different explanation of what has happened in the last few days, and is happening now as these words are spoken. Common sense tells Stéphane Moineaux that none of this is real, and that everything that he has seen or heard since the silly accident that ran a sword into his breast is just a dream, experienced in the brief interval that separates life and the afterlife, while I am lying prostrate behind this curtain, having died on stage once too often.

"In speaking to you as Stéphane Moineaux, however, I also have to add that I have never been an admirer of that exotic alloy common sense, which has always seemed to me to have far too much in it that is common and far too little that is sense. As a gentleman of the theater, I have always favored uncommon sense and the imp of the perverse, and however unlikely it might seem that reality is mimicking a dream rather than *vice versa*, that is the preferable alternative on aesthetic grounds, and it is the one I choose. In either case, of course, I would have to play my part to the full, but it is infinitely better to play one's part as a creature of flesh and blood, however frail, on a real stage, than it is to do it as a ghost of the imagination in the phantom spaces of the mind. So I offer one more promise, as much to myself as to you: this melodrama is real, solid, and tangible; it is life, and because it is the kind of life that struts upon a stage in a theater, it is also art.

"Because this melodrama is art as well as life, there is yet another possible explanation of what has happened during these last few days, and what is happening now. Those members of the audience who are writers themselves–who constitute a considerable constituency, thanks to the heroic efforts of my good friend Monsieur Jarry–will be very familiar with the manner in which authentic works of art take on a life of their own, equipping themselves as they grow with their own aesthetic imperatives. I, as a mere actor and director, cannot presume to speak for all those writers, or even to assume that they would agree among themselves, but I suspect that some of them, at least, will understand what I mean when I say that this play, more than any other that I have ever had the privilege to produce, has taken on a life of its own. In so doing, it has imposed its own aesthetic imperatives on its cast, with a compulsive force rarely witnessed on the Parisian stage.

"Although I do not believe in curses or forcible diabolical pacts–or that if the Devil did exist, he would ever consent to manifest himself in the strange and petty fashion of an unlooked-for riposte in a fugitive dramatic production, when the same trick might be used to slay archbishops or emperors–I do believe in art. I do believe in *the magic of the theater*, and that is why I feel entitled to suggest to you that the agency responsible for what has happened in this theater during the last few nights might have been the play itself, asserting its prerogatives in spite of the best efforts of its author, its director and its actors. That, at least, was the basis on which I formulated my plan to solve the problem with which I and my company were confronted.

"There was a period of time–at least an hour, and perhaps half a day–as I lay in my hospital bed, sometimes seemingly asleep and sometimes seemingly awake, when I contemplated letting *Le Nouveau Faust* continue as it had begun. I knew that I would never run short of volunteers to play the part that I took tonight, no matter how many of them might fall down dead in exactly the same fashion as the unfortunate Comte de Farineux. I knew that playing the part would become the ultimate challenge, which no honorable swordsman could refuse, even if he had no confidence that he could win. The prospect of facing the supernatural riposte that injured me and killed two other men would have been an irresistible lure to men of a certain kind: brave, proud, ambitious men, ready and willing to spit in the Devil's eye no matter what the cost.

"There are a great many such men in existence today, just as there were in 1804. You and I, ladies and gentlemen, have lived our entire lives in an era replete with such men: a Faustian era, not in the intended sense of the original *Faust-buch*, which painted Faust as a wicked man deserving of damnation by virtue of unholy ambition, but in the sense of *Le Nouveau Faust*, which depicts Jean Faust as a hero whose damnation would be an intolerable tragedy. You will doubtless have remarked that I did not say *Simon de Keramour*'s *Le Nouveau Faust*, because that is not *Le Nouveau Faust* to which I refer. I mean the true *Le Nouveau Faust*, which has made its bid for freedom, independence and self-determination: *Le Nouveau Faust* that came within a centimeter of striking me dead on Saturday night, and made no mistake with my luckless understudy and the valiant Comte de Farineux.

"When I say that *Le Nouveau Faust* attempted to strike me dead, I do not mean that it attempted to strike me dead in my capacity of actor-manager. I do not believe that it regarded Stéphane Moineaux as its enemy, although it might conceivably have had its suspicions about my effectiveness as an ally. The person that it intended to strike dead was its own character–it's own *unsatisfactory* character–and the reason it attempted to perform that essentially-surgical act was that it knew full well that Mephistopheles ought not to win the climactic duel. It knew full well that Faust ought to be the victor, and that was the end that it was trying to achieve.

"When I first saw the need for the ending of the play to be changed, I immediately happened upon the possibility that the identity-exchange might be reversed once the duel was complete, but I did not extrapolate the argument to its logical conclusion. I thought, at first, of changing the outcome of the duel, so that the character played by the younger actor would recover from his apparent death while the character played by the older actor should perish in his stead–but I took it for granted that the younger actor should resume the part of Mephistopheles rather than retaining the role of Faust. I rejected the idea, but I rejected it for the wrong reasons. I rejected it because I–meaning Stéphane Moineaux–had no intention of surrendering the final scene to my *jeune premier*. Having rejected it once, I thought no more about it while the play was in rehearsal–and that was where my mistake lay.

"What I should have done, as has now become obvious, was to preserve the result of the duel as it as scripted, but deny that the identity-exchange had ever really taken place, so that I, as Stéphane Moineaux, could win as Jean Faust, and not as Mephistopheles. The play knew that, and had to make it clear to me–but the only way it could do that was by delivering an indirect prompt: by showing me the outcome of a victory for Faust as represented by the wrong actor. I am truly sorry that it took me so long to glimpse the natural solution, and to act upon it. I have done so now, and have explained the why of it if not the what. That is why I am so confident in assuring you that the play has now fulfilled its urge to progress, at least for the time being. Its evolution has been diverted on to the right path, and although it will never cease to change, it has the right momentum and vital spirit. It will not kill again.

"I must confess, though, as I find myself experiencing increasing difficulty in winding up this speech, that I do not know how much my effort has cost me. It is possible that the strain I have put on the injury to my heart has opened the cut more widely, and that I am bleeding to death internally. It is also possible that the strain has aggravated a latent infection, which is now poisoning my blood and driving up my bodily temperature to an unsustainable level. If either of those circumstances is realized, then I shall not be here tomorrow to play the role of *Le Nouveau Faust*—but there is no need to worry that the play will revert to its murderous tendencies in my absence, for there is an amanuensis scribbling away furiously somewhere close at hand. Whoever takes my place will play my part as I have played it, conserving the drama's final victory for flawed humankind rather than rehabilitated demonkind.

"Whether I can retain the part of Faust or not, I can assure you that Simon de Keramour will not retain the part of Mephistopheles, which will in future be played by the actor for whom it was initially designed, and for whom it will surely provide the platform for a great career: Paul Damas. I say that not because I believe that Simon de Keramour is dead, having been fatally wounded by my blade or having fractured his skull when he fell, but simply because it is the right casting decision.

"Monsieur de Keramour once said to me that his play would only be altered *over his dead body*, but I cannot believe that *Le Nouveau Faust* would take him literally—he is, after all, its progenitor. This is *Le Nouveau Faust* we are talking about, not *Oedipus Rex*. When you saw the blood spurt from Mephistopheles' breast a few moments ago, it was a merely a *coup de théâtre* produced by a cunningly-placed blood-bag, and when you heard his head strike the stage, it was merely the sound of a man being knocked unconscious. He will wake up, ladies and gentleman, in the hospital, where Doctor Emile Louvois' generous and expert care will put him right in no time.

"You might perhaps think that in making such a guarantee, I am exceeding my warrant as a character and as a director, but whether I am Jean Faust or Stéphane Moineaux, or some chimerical combination of the two, I am still *in the play*, and therefore privy to its secrets. *Le Nouveau Faust* never intended to kill its author. When it was finally allowed to come out *right*, with the ends of modern poetic justice properly served, it did not want to kill its Mephistopheles either. Quite the reverse, in fact, for a good play is at least as moral as a good man, and likely to be far more generous in its particular dispositions. A play–even a humble melodrama in which tragedy and comedy are chimerically juxtaposed, in order to draw narrative energy from their contradiction–is a work of art, and the whole *raison d'être* of a work of art is to be generous in supplying audiences with food for thought and pleasurable confections, all bound up in a gourmet gastronomic experience.

"Some of you, I know, might be slightly disappointed to know that there will be no further fatal accidents at the Tragicomique–not, at least, on a nightly basis–because the modern appetite for sensation is sometimes left unsated by mere stageblood, even in the quantities deployed with such lavish cleverness just around the corner, at the Grand Guignol. The writers among you will know, however, that effective artifice is always and infinitely to be preferred to unscripted actuality, most especially where matters of violence and suffering are concerned; I hope that the other members of the audience may, in time, be able to see the force of that argument. If not, I doubt that the world that is now in gestation will leave them short of opportunities to experience real bloodshed and suffering, on a scale unheralded in any work of art. Jean Faust's metaphorical victory has its darker implications–necessarily so, given that all the brighter lights set out for our guidance cast darker shadows.

"There may also be some among you, even among the writers invited by Monsieur Jarry, who will think that this entire speech is a product of fever, if not of insanity. Perhaps they are right; if I were insane, I would not know it, and I have never been the sort of artist who takes grateful refuge in the vulgar opinion that genius is closely allied and inevitably alloyed with madness. I would be lying if I told you that the thought had been entirely banished from my mind that I have dreamed everything that seems to have happened since I was struck unconscious on *Le Nouveau Faust*'s opening night. I can only repeat, though, that the reality of all of this–the theater, the stage, the play, the suspense that is tangible in the atmosphere–is by far the preferable hypothesis, on aesthetic grounds. I beg you, therefore, to credit me with fervor rather than fever, and artistry if not with sanity.

"Having said all that, I ought perhaps to conclude by offering some implication of closure, if not a formal moral. Some of the writers among you might think that I ought to say something about the outcome of Jean Faust's experiment in diabolical enlightenment, and its relevance to contemporary humankind. Others would doubtless feel that the outcome of the play's action ought to speak for itself, as action always speaks more loudly than words. I shall attempt a compromise by saying this: that the true central character of *Le Nouveau Faust*, as in every other literary version of Faust, is not Faust at all but the human symbol of his complex and confused desires, here represented–in a cunningly contrived dual role–by the actress who has progressed herein from *ingénue* to heroine: Lillette Fevret.

"Simon de Keramour's notes to the script describe one of Lillette's guises as a personification of lust, but he might as well have done the same for both, for the essence of her character is the conflict generated by the lust for knowledge and the lust for sensation, between intellect and sensuality. Some of you, at least, come to the Tragicomique simply to admire Lillette's beauty, and you are right to do so–but those who call it the Devil's beauty are simply wrong, for it is a better kind of beauty altogether. I could go on, but I sense that I am about to fall down now, because I can no longer hold myself upright. Lillette, who is doubtless waiting in the wings for her cue, will rush out to ascertain whether I am alive or dead. Apart from calling for a stretcher to bear me away, she has no lines to deliver, but she will look up from my body, and out into the auditorium, so that you will be able to obtain the full benefit of the sight of her tearful face. That will be enough, ladies and gentlemen, to provide *Le Nouveau Faust* with its perfect coda. Look back at her, ladies and gentlemen, and remember both aspects of her character. Look at her, and try to see her beauty as the reflection of your own best dreams–and be glad that you were here tonight at the Théâtre Tragicomique, to see a performance whose like has never been seen before upon the Paris stage."

Then, as he had predicted, the man on the stage collapsed.

Lillette Fevret came running from the wings to bend over him anxiously. She called for a stretcher–and then she looked up and out into the auditorium, to display her tearful face in the dazzling lights.

The applause was thunderous. It continued for a long time after Stéphane Moineaux's inert body had been carried away.

24

Stéphane Moineaux peeped out from between his almost-closed eyelids, waiting for his pupils to adapt so that he could determine where he was and who was with him. He knew that there were other people present because it was the sound of their conversation that had awakened him.

There was no sign of Dürer or Callot in the background; instead the wall on the far side of the set bore painted posters representing Stéphane Moineaux as the English Milord in *Le Vampire* and as the eponymous caliph in William Beckford's *Vathek*. He was obviously at home, in his own bed.

There were three old and well-worn chairs dawn up beside the bed. The one nearest the bed-head was occupied by Lillette Fevret. Paul Damas was sat next to her with Marianne Jonquille on his far side. Doctor Emile Louvois was standing

183

behind Lillette, looking down at his patient, evidently slightly uncomfortable in these strange surroundings.

Moineaux ran his tongue around his mouth and sucked on it to increase the flow of saliva; he did not want his opening line to sound unduly hoarse. One of the conversationalists observed his movement and told the others that he was waking up. The chatter lapsed, and the entire audience waited with rapt attention as he raised his eyelids a little further.

"What day is it?" he demanded.

"Thursday," said Paul Damas.

"And how long have I been asleep?"

"Eleven hours, *Maître*–ever since you collapsed on stage after making your speech to conclude last night's performance. It's a quarter to ten in the morning."

Moineaux permitted himself a sigh of relief. "I knew it was real, really," he said, by way of self-justification.

"You are, of course assuming that you really have woken up," Paul pointed out. "If you were still asleep, this might merely be a extension of your hallucination–or your eternal punishment."

"Please don't confuse my patient," Louvois put in. "He's had quite enough stress lately without being required to deal with ridiculous conundrums. I am quite real, Monsieur Moineaux, even though I am not usually to be found so far from the hospital. All of this is real, as any good positivist would be delighted to reassure you."

Moineaux brought his right hand out from beneath the coverlet and looked at Lillette. "Would you take my hand, if you please, my dear?" he said. "And would you kiss me, very gently, on the forehead."

The ex-*ingénue* took his gnarled hand in her own delicate fingers. She leaned forward and kissed him, with the utmost propriety, on the forehead.

"That solves one of your problems, Paul," Moineaux declared. "I'm certainly not in Hell."

"There was a time when you'd have asked me to do that, Stéphane," Marianne observed, bitterly. "Am I invisible now, or merely irrelevant? May I remind you that I'm a year younger than Sarah Bernhardt, and still very handsome?"

"And that solves the other," Moineaux said. "This is definitely real, for I could never dream of finding you so angry on discovering that I am still alive. Is my life still in danger, doctor? I must say that I feel quite well."

"There might be some residual risk," Louvois told him, "but you haven't bled to death, and your fever was due to over-exertion rather than bacterial infection. If you consent to obey my instructions this time, I hope and expect that you'll be up and about by the weekend."

"Nonsense!" Moineaux exclaimed. "I'll be up and about by three o'clock. I have a part to rehearse. Did the amanuensis copy down my speech?"

"Every word," Paul told him. "Does it matter? If your promises meant anything, we'll surely be able to revert to the ending in the script now, playing the last scene as Monsieur de Keramour intended."

"Imbecile!" Moineaux said. "We have our ending–the play and I have seen to that. I don't say that it won't need a little tinkcring, and a certain amount of refinement, but we certainly have our ending. Even Simon de Keramour must agree to that. Where is he, by the way?"

"He's lying in the room at the hospital that was yours until last night," Louvois told him. "He's not seriously injured, but I'd like to keep him there until I'm satisfied that there's no residual concussion."

"Messieurs Dürer and Callot will keep him company," Moineaux declared, lightly, "and he'll appreciate the dim lighting far more than I ever did. Have you been given permission to play your part tonight, Paul?"

"I have," the *jeune premier* confirmed. "The prosecutor confirmed an hour ago that he will take no action against me, and that I am at liberty to do as I will. I'm not so sure, though, that Simon will be any more content to remain in the hospital than you were–and he won't take very kindly to his play being so drastically rewritten. He didn't hear your speech, you know, or the applause that followed it."

"He has no alternative but to let us play it as we please," Marianne observed. "It's a sensational success, and all the credit for that is being given to Monsieur Moineaux. Were he to withdraw it, he'd be hunted down by a mob–and if he takes it to another theater, no director will touch it without permission to use Monsieur Moineaux's ending instead of his."

"Monsieur de Keramour might not have heard my speech *consciously*," Moineaux said, "but I'm certain that *Le Nouveau Faust* will get through to him, as it got through to me. With luck, he'll be able to work on rewriting the script for Lavinière's copy-typists while he's in Doctor Louvois' tender care. In the meantime, we'll get by with what we have. We've proved that we can do it—haven't we, Lillette?"

"I never imagined that I could be so inventive," Lillette said, "but now that I know, I shan't fail. So long as I'm playing opposite you, *Maître*, I shall be able to improvise my scenes with the utmost conviction."

"Quite so," Moineaux agreed. "You were brilliant, my dear, quite brilliant–and you will be even more brilliant in future. How many luxurious carriages were queued up at the stage door last night–and which lucky man had the privilege of taking you home?"

"At least a dozen," she told him, "including Monsieur Léchelier's–but I walked home, escorted by Monsieur France and Monsieur Huysmans. I bid them goodnight on my doorstep. They were very gallant, and very polite. I shall have to move to new lodgings, of course, since my old ones were rented by the late Comte. I'm sorry about what happened to him–so sorry, I think, that I don't think it would be appropriate to rush into a similar relationship. I think I might concentrate on improving my art by myself for a while. I shall need an increase in salary, of course."

"So will I," Paul put in. "Forty francs a month..."

"I'll need at least 60," Lillette said.

"And you shall have them," Moineaux assured them, "just as soon as the Tragicomique is safe from bankruptcy, and not a moment later. That shouldn't take long, given our new fashionability. Mind you, Lillette, Simon de Keramour is sure to lay siege to your affections, no matter how skillfully you feign mourning. Writers have no sense of proportion in romantic matters, and they can never believe that their objects of adoration are less romantic than themselves."

"He's a gentleman," Lillette said, blithely. "He won't be a nuisance–and he'll stand guard over me in the green room, if necessary."

"If you're wise, Stéphane," Marianne said, "you'll give me full authority over the day-to-day running of the theater until you're fully recovered, especially if you intend playing your part every night. It won't be easy, you know–you're still wounded."

"I've played Molière with a migraine," Moineaux reminded her, "and Féval with a fever–not once, but 50 times over. I'm indestructible. But you're right. You have my authority to represent me in all merely worldly matters, until Doctor Louvois is convinced that I am well. You may have a modest increase in salary by way of recompense–but not until the theater is safe from bankruptcy."

"Audiences might begin to lose interest, once we have played for a month or two without anyone getting hurt," Paul observed.

"I doubt that," Moineaux said. "There will always be the *possibility* that someone might get hurt–and the play, as presently reconstituted, is surely irresistible to any true aficionado of the theater."

"It's very complicated," Marianne observed.

"And very eccentric," Paul added.

"But it ends well," Lillette supplied.

"I wasn't present at your performance last night, Monsieur Moineaux," Emile Louvois put in, "but I've heard numerous reports of what you said after the curtain fell. As a good positivist, I approve wholeheartedly of your frank denial that a curse or the Devil had anything to do with the series of misfortunes that afflicted your production, but I'm not sure that I can approve of your speaking of a play as if it were an entity capable of independent motivation and agency. A play is just a series of lines, scribbled or spoken. It has no life of its own."

"All the world's a stage, doctor," Moineaux told him, "and every human being within it but a player, improvising lines as best he–or she–can. I doubt that history and destiny have a playwright, but I don't doubt for a moment that there *is* a play, with its own inherent aesthetic logic. We're free to name ourselves as we will, and to invent our lines as we can, but still we must operate within the framework of that play. There are narrative moves we cannot make–not, at least, without placing ourselves in dire peril of injury and death–and there are narrative moves that we *must* make, for art's sake."

"Even so..." the doctor began–but Moineaux was now wide awake and in full flow, and would not tolerate interruption.

"To be or not to be is *not* the question," the great actor-manager went on, relentlessly. "The question is *what* to be, and how to achieve it–how to *play one's part*. The only sane alternative to suffering the slings and arrows of outrageous fortune is to armor oneself against them as best one can. Don't you agree, my dear?"

"Yes," Lillette Fevret and Marianne Jonquille said, simultaneously.

"You ought to have an amanuensis close at hand all the time, to write all your speeches down," Paul remarked. "I know that your memory's good, and exceedingly well-trained, but think what a loss it would be to the world if some of the gems you scatter so liberally were lost for lack of a loyal scribbler."

"Please don't be sarcastic, Paul," Moineaux said. "You'll give me a headache. I think you ought to go now–all of you. We'll start the rehearsal at three."

"This will be the most intensively-reworked play in history," Marianne observed. "No two performances alike in its first week. I may be a little younger than the divine Sarah, but I'm too old for all this. Thank God my part is one that hardly changes at all."

"There is no God," said the Comtean doctor, decisively, "and it's high time that we lost the indolent habit of referring to him, let alone the unnecessary folly of thanking Him."

"You were bound to say that, doctor," Moineaux told him. "That's the part you're playing, and can't escape it–but you needn't stick quite so religiously to the script. Your presence on stage is hardly necessary now, though. I need to rest–perhaps to sleep, perchance to dream."

The three players got up, obediently, and followed the doctor to the door.

"Three o'clock, *Maître*," Lillette said.

"I'll be there," Moineaux promised. "Old melodramatists never die, and if they ever do, they invariably come back from the grave as troublesome spirits. The Tragicomique will never be rid of me. I'll be there, today and every day, to play my part."

If any proof were needed that the once-famous actor had now become an oracle, on whose predictions everyone could rely, that night provided it, and every night thereafter. The play went on, and on. Like its new Faust, the Tragicomique was saved.